"**L**eo!" I shouted. "Gun!" I spared a hung half out of her passenger of us!"

Leo passed me his machine gun while Olivia returned to her seat. Looking forward she shouted, "Zut alors, Doran!" Damn it, Doran, in French.

Rolling down my window, I took the machine gun in a one-handed grip and thrust it outside. Without taking the time to aim, I depressed the trigger. The roar filled the cab of the car more than Olivia's little pistol did. It was so loud that I didn't even hear Olivia's shooting, although I could see that she was miming me with her own gun.

The Nazis ahead of us scattered, diving behind their jeeps and off the road. I didn't slow the car at all and rammed the two jeeps that were blocking the road. Olivia and I managed to bring our guns in only barely in time and avoided losing our arms. In the backseat Leo was releasing a long string of curses.

Only a few of the soldiers had the wherewithal to remember that they were supposed to be stopping us and continued to shoot as they dove out of the way. The shots were mostly wide with only a few hitting the doors and the trunk. A loud sound of metal sliding across metal hit my ears next and holler of victory from Leo confirmed that we'd also lost our tail.

The Statement of Andrew Doran

by MATTHEW DAVENPORT

Special thanks to Kelsey!

Chapter 1: Miskatonic University

The sun beat down on me with a ferocity that I'd only seen before in the boxing matches. This form of punishment had taken me completely by surprise. This surprise had lost its edge about three hours previously, and I was long since past caring about it.

My initial surprise was due to the nature of the execution. I was being hanged by my wrists in the Mexico sun and I was naked. This was completely out of character for the Night Watchers, the midnight tribe. An offshoot of the Aztec that managed to survive their collapse, the Night Watchers had taken to the worship of Night Gaunts, man shaped horrors with no faces and large bat-like wings. The Night Gaunts were known in most cultures as mythical beasts that would ride the darkness between reality and dreams. The Night Gaunts were to blame when people failed to come back to the waking world, having instead been devoured in the Dream Lands.

So, to be strung up in the sun is an intriguing way to die, given the circumstances.

As I'd mentioned previously, the surprise was quickly put to the back of my mind as I struggled to reverse my unfortunate situation. That was three hours ago. I hadn't given up.

I like to think that I had decided to internalize my struggles.

Pressing my mind to the furthest reaches of my being, I was trying to use the teachings found in the "dreaded" book by that fool Arab. In the past, under ideal conditions, I'd managed to enter the Dream Lands, and even once found that I could affect the walls of reality from there.

Sadly, I wasn't as mad as the Arab yet, and was a little too distracted by the sunburn on my more indecent regions. Surrendering, I opened my eyes, and looked down at my bright red feet. As I stared at them, only bringing more attention to the pain, I got my first real surprise in three hours.

It felt that the shadow stared at me for as long as I stared at it. My eyes kept at the shadow cast on my feet for what seemed like an eternity before it spoke to me.

"Andrew Doran?"

"That's Doctor Andrew Doran," I croaked out. I obviously hadn't completely surrendered. I'd earned that doctorate, and I'd be damned if I'd die without it.

"Yes, well, Dr. Doran then." The voice was educated and, judging by the shoes that had fallen into my vision, not prepared for the climate. "I am Dr. Stoll. Benjamin Stoll, and I've come to return you to Miskatonic."

This had to be a hallucination. My mind was finally breaking and creating the most preposterous of circumstances. Next my very beard would be crawling up my face to start a chat with my eyelids.

I hadn't been back to Miskatonic University in almost ten years. This was mostly due to them banning me, but also because of my stubborn attitude. Miskatonic thought itself the center of all educational fronts and shunned looking too deeply into the texts they label forbidden, but that archaeology labels necessary.

They had become a bunch of tired, old zealots who coveted their books and shared their real knowledge with no man.

We shall refer to it as 'mutual disinterest.' And yes, I am an alumni. It's a more sordid past than with any lady I've ever met.

I finally used the last of my strength to raise my chin from my chest. This created a cascade of fire over the back of my neck that threatened to steal my very senses. The energy to let my eyes examine his gave the image of a man slowly sizing him up. At least I hope that it did.

Dr. Benjamin Stoll was bald, completely, and so pale that I figured him to burn up as I watched him. He was dressed in a full grey suit, complete with jacket. He had thin wire framed glasses and a thick mustache that put my beard to shame. It took my sunbathed brain a minute or two to comprehend, but he wasn't sweating, and he wasn't even red. I'm most likely the most traveled man to ever graduate from that cursed school and would normally take the time to place his clothing, his dialect, even his lineage based on physical characteristics. In this instance, there was no need.

"Miskatonic sent you? You mean the Department of Archaeology sent you. Why send a shoggoth when the sun would have done the job for you?"

The man-shaped monster smiled. "While consuming your essence would satisfy me beyond your comprehension, I have been compelled, via the means at Miskatonic's disposal, to invite you to Miskatonic for a discussion. Sending myself is meant to be an indication towards the urgency of the request." He kept smiling, as if he forgot how to stop, and reached out and over my head. I hadn't seen a blade, and he obviously hadn't exerted himself. It was a shoggoth displaying his inhuman characteristics to a man in no place to do that which came normally to him.

I've made it my occupation to kill the soul sucking shoggoths and all their ilk from the Necronomicon. Being aided by one disgusts me, but a slight smile found my burned and tired face as I knew that the Earth's sun wasn't healthy for a shoggoth. As a matter of fact, Dr. Stoll probably felt as burnt up as I did.

On top of all my deep-seated hate for his kind, Dr. Stoll had also been sent by that damned school to collect me. As if I would ever be in their employ.

I no sooner hit the ground than I raised my weakened hands and shouted in a harsh voice "Cthalgn Flthagnic!" It was mostly a bunch of crossed consonants with a vowel or two mixed together. It sounded like a phlegm-y barking cough and this was only made more cough-like by my sunbaked voice.

These were words, though. Ancient and all powerful words that came directly from the book of the Necronomicon, and as with all knowledge gained from that book, it had come to serve me well over the years.

Darkness leapt from my hands and engulfed the shoggoth, and all about his body came a stiffening and a final shudder as he found that he could no longer move.

The effort sapped the last of my strength and I collapsed to the baked earth, unable to even lift my head.

Shoggoths, as with every monster and beastie in the Necronomicon, didn't need mouths to talk and this one was chattier than my beloved sister.

Release me. You will not be able to leave this desert in your current condition. I have been compelled and am incapable of killing you. You will be safe with me.

Of course, the monster was right. We were hundreds of miles from civilization and the magics of the shoggoth could get me anywhere safer than here, but my hate for the evils that prey on mankind, no matter how *domesticated*, knew no bounds. From my prone position, I squeezed my fist, tightening my magical grip on the beast. This last effort drained me even further, and I dropped my head to the sand. Without looking, I could feel my spell snap as the shoggoth broke my ever-weakening grasp.

In the matter of an instant, I was at eye-level with the monster, but I was not upright. A slimy shadow had tentacled out of the monster's human abdomen and spiraled around my body, holding me upside down.

You are food, and somewhere in the long line of your being food, you and your people have forgotten your place. You are known to us, Dr. Andrew Doran. We call you the Klgthorf. It has no equivalent in your mind, but the closest I can come to a translation would be 'the cockroach that bites.' You are insects to us, and you, Dr. Doran, above all of the other cockroaches, are in dire need of a lesson.

During this intrusion into my mind, he'd begun absorbing my soul through his contact with me. He couldn't kill me, as he'd said previously, but it didn't stop him from taking a sip.

Even this close to death, you have so much … soul….

Through gritted teeth I said, "Enjoy the taste and take note of its flavor. You're going to find something hidden underneath my strong survival sense. That's steel determination. Compelled or not, I will kill you and all your kind." I spat as I said lastly, "Taste my *conviction!*"

The facial expressions of a shoggoth in human form are impossible to read on the best of days. They've never taken the time to learn our mannerisms, and why should they? We don't take the time to learn a cow's mannerisms as we're eating a juicy steak. Years of hunting them, killing them, and running from them, had taught me to look for little tells, and as the shoggoth drank from me, I saw one of these clues. His entire image wavered. His mind had been hit by a strong enough surprise that he'd let his grip on his projected illusion slip, just for a second. I saw him then, as I always saw him, but also with my eyes. He was a perfect specimen of a disgusting species; a collection of mouths and tentacles all drifting in an amorphous blob of some dark and oily substance.

Those many mouths had tasted my soul and he'd been scared by what he had found.

Painfully, I was on the ground again, and before I could do anything to object, the shoggoth had reached down and touched my forehead with cold, imaginary, man-hands. In that moment, we were transported across space and through the void between distances.

The nightmares of the mind dwell in the void, and I did my best to keep my mind's eye closed during the trip, but I was far too weak to keep all the horrors out. We landed in a library with a high ceiling and several chairs. The smell of a cigar touched my nostrils and reminded me of something that I couldn't place. Something dark and invasive from my split-second trip in the void. I was shivering from the trip, not from the cold as it looked to be surprisingly warm in the New England town of Arkham.

"Shoggoths: you can dress them up, compel them to do your dirty work, but they don't have the common decency to dress a man before dropping his naked self in my library."

I don't like to beat around the bush, and I had no energy to jump up and punch Dean Brandon Smythe in his smug mouth, so I spoke my mind. "Smythe," I spat. "You're messing with monsters as if they were puppies. This one is going to break his leash, and I hope I'm there to watch him flay you alive."

The Dean crouched before me and looked me in the eyes. "Yes, well, it's good to see you haven't lost your bark." He touched my chin and I felt dirtier than three hours in the desert sun and being touched by a shoggoth had made me. "If you've finished being disagreeable, I'd like to get you cleaned up and dressed, at which point I'd like to explain why we didn't just let you die in the desert. Is this agreeable?"

I grunted, and he must have accepted it as an affirmative. I wasn't sure if it was, but I wanted pants, and a very cold shower. Besides Miskatonic has always had something I wanted and I w~~ ˙ to pass up a chance to finally get my hands on it, . remote that chance was.

I don't remember how I got from the library to the shower, and that's probably for the best. The void holds very little for the sane man, and while I'd confronted things more sanity shattering than the void in the past, I'm normally less weak and sun baked when I face them.

I was dressed in a plain button up shirt and brown trousers. It was my normal attire before I'd gone to live with the Night Watchers, and as loathe as I was to be in Miskatonic, it was a nostalgic feeling of comfort that came over me as I dressed.

I looked myself over in the mirror and was surprised to see that I didn't look nearly as bad as I felt. My thick mop of brown hair had been cut short before my self-induced insanity to become one of the Night Watchers and then destroy them from within, but that was over a month ago, and it had returned to its more unruly nature.

I took a comb to it and managed to make it decent enough before turning the comb and clippers to my beard. I'm a firm believer that a trimmed beard is the only sign that humanity still has hope, and took my time with this.

Twenty minutes after I'd left the library, I'd made my way back down there, without the aid of the shoggoth. I'll always take my own feet over void travel.

Smythe hadn't left the library, and as I walked back in he was sitting and flipping through a book.

Dean Brandon Smythe was the embodiment of the tired, old zealots running their vault of knowledge. He was clean shaven and bald except for wisps of hair that he combed from one side of his broad head to the other. He was old, but not old enough to have been replaced yet, although I had heard that he'd chosen a successor.

In regards to the book he wasn't really paying attention to, it wasn't lost on me that this wasn't just any book. Smythe was holding the only reason I was willing to contemplate going along with whatever dirty work that Miskatonic's Department of Archaeology had concocted this time.

In Smythe's hands was the only English translation of the Necronomicon. Miskatonic University had acquired it in 1918, more than twenty years ago. This translated version was the most up-to-date edition, and included the most detailed practices by those Dagon worshippers of the Polynesian islands, and the largest collection of transliterated spells for summonings and banishments. This was the most complete text on the creatures that preyed on humanity, and therefore the best possible weapon in my arsenal against them.

Part of my anger with all Miskatonic, and especially Dean Smythe, was that this Necronomicon was on public display in the library. Every couple of months, someone of shifty morals, or maybe someone who was just a little curious, would crack open the book and cause mayhem that would inevitably give the horrors of our world and the next more ground in our reality.

I emphasize *our* reality. They have their own and they are invaders, pushing into our world to cause horrors unimaginable.

Some information should be guarded and protected from the ignorant and instead made a tool by someone who would know how to responsibly make use of it. I wanted this book, for me and to keep it from them.

It was no coincidence that he was reading that book at the moment I had chosen to come down, but I opted to ignore it. He knew I wanted it, and it wouldn't be long before he offered it, falsely, for whatever he asked me to do.

"Thank you for the shower and clothes." I nodded towards where the shoggoth hid, invisible, in the corner of the room. In my chosen occupation, one of the first things that you learn is that once you've seen beyond the veil, you can't unsee what's been seen. "And thank you for saving my life." I looked directly into the Dean's eyes. "Now tell me what you want so that I can spit into your face for a specific reason."

"All the charm as usual, Doctor." Smythe threw the Necronomicon he'd been thumbing through at my chest where I caught it and held it, not removing my eyes from him. I held my newly formed anger deep within me, trying not to let it add to the fire that Smythe had already earned. He just threw a *book*. Added to that sacrilege was the flair of my sunburned chest and hands as I caught the book.

"Oh, would you stop being stone cold angry long enough to hear what has to be said. Look at the damned book."

I tore my eyes from his and looked down at the book. I chose to stop hiding my anger instantly.

The cover was in German. Flipping through the pages, I found that every page was written in German. This wasn't my English edition of the famed book. This was German. Either the University had acquired a second copy of the very rare book or…

"You let the Nazis take the book." I said it through gritted teeth.

Smythe crossed his legs and took out a small swath of cloth. "Nobody let anybody take anything. It was stolen." Taking off his glasses, he calmly cleaned them as he said, "Go ahead and say the 'I told you so' so that we can move forward and get to fixing the problem."

"You son of a bitch. You self-righteous asshole." I hadn't needed his permission, but I saw no reason not to oblige. "For years, I've petitioned you to at least hide the book securely in one of your many vaults. If you can't bring yourself to destroy it, then lock it up! No, instead you keep it in a very public room, in front of children." I hesitated, letting my words sink in to both of us. I was angry and I almost told him that I'd go find it, just like he wanted me to. I allowed myself a chance to cool down, but I didn't let it into my face at all. "Enjoy fixing this one. I won't have a part in it."

Dean Smythe put his glasses gently back onto his face. "Well, now that we've gotten that out of the way…" He stood up and stuck his hand out to me, as if I would ever shake his hand. "So, you'll go get the book and then we'll let you borrow it under the conditions that after one year we shove it into the deepest vault known to exist."

He'd played every card he had. That was almost the exact words I used in my letter to him ten years ago demanding that he hand over the book. He was giving me everything I wanted and he knew I couldn't refuse it. "I'll need help getting into Germany."

He nodded and lowered his hand, understanding that I wouldn't touch him. "That's easy, we've got hoggoths."

I suppressed a shudder at the thought of the void travel. "Weapons?" I knew Brandon Smythe, Dean of Miskatonic University, wouldn't give me any guns, but Smythe also knew that guns were the furthest thing from my mind.

"Borrow or own?"

"Depends on if I like it." I shrugged.

He nodded slowly. "Then I won't show you my favorites."

It was my turn to nod, turning my palm over slowly and generating a ball of flame in my palm. It was a simple trick, and not worth anything in a fight, but I was betting that Smythe didn't know that. "I wouldn't show you the fine china either."

I sensed the shoggoth move and I could tell that Smythe couldn't. The shoggoth knew what kind of weapons we meant, and I doubt that Smythe had ever been quite dumb enough to have told it where the armory was.

Of course, I meant supernatural weapons. Talismans to protect, buckles to banish, and blades that dispel.

Smythe dug into his pocket and whispered something under his breath. He pulled out a dirty coin, plain and not special by any means, but I could sense the static energy coming off it. He'd placed an incantation onto it.

"This coin will lead you to the Miskatonic Armory. If you feel that you're being followed," the Dean looked over his shoulder, but not towards the shoggoth at all, even though that was his target, "dispatch your pursuer by any means that you see fit."

I held back from laughing right in the Dean's face. He'd just threatened a monster that he couldn't even find in a locked room. I silently hoped that I'd be there to watch as the monster devoured his soul.

I pocketed the coin, tossed the German Necronomicon on a chair, and started for the door that I had entered through. I stopped before touching the door handle and turned to look one last time into Dean Brandon Smythe's old eyes. I wanted to see his smug look one last time and remind him that he didn't own me.

"Don't let my cooperation go to your head, Smythe. I'm only doing this for the book, not for you. Never for you."

"You're cooperating for the same reason you do everything: from some false belief that you can protect mankind from these things. You're bailing water when you should be jumping ship." He held up his hands in a placating gesture. "Whatever helps you swallow it, Dr. Doran. You're a monster killer, you'll continue to work for me as long as I provide you monsters."

I smiled, and I like to think that he saw murder in my eyes then. "Or until I decide that you *are* one."

I had used coin magics before, and finding the armory was a simple matter. Coin magic, in its variants, is location magic. When I'm facing the wrong direction the coin gets hotter and is at its hottest when I'm facing directly away from my target.

Simple magic, but nonetheless effective. It took me to a large wall painting in an area of the building that looked somehow related to the mathematics wing of Miskatonic University. I slowly turned on my heels a few times to ensure that the painting was the correct spot and then pocketed the coin quickly, hiding the movement from eyes that might be prying.

Before giving any movements towards entering the hidden armory, I opened my senses. Reaching around me, I felt with my mind towards the corners and around the turns of the hallway. Not only searching for shoggoths, but for any errant magics or beings. Miskatonic's collection of books and weapons (in any library the two are indistinguishable, and even more so at Miskatonic) is extensive, and I wouldn't doubt that all sorts of monsters, otherworldly beings, or fraternity boys would be dying to get their hands on some artifact or relic.

It'd do no good to enter a hidden armory only to be watched while doing it.

Deciding that the coast was clear, I pulled the coin back from my pocket and raised it to the painting. The image was of some Brown Jenkin, a rat bodied monster with a man's face, dragging a dead man's detached arm through some sewer grate in a far removed basement. The artistry was too realistic, and I could feel the eyes of the Brown Jenkin peeking directly at me, wondering when he might get a chance to take my arm into whatever nether regions he called home.

This was obviously the work of Richard Upton Pickman. Some claimed him to be a man, but I was sure he wasn't wholly of this world. Pickman claimed that the imagery of the paintings came to him in his dreams, but there have been some accounts that the imagery was that of living models. This painting, as far as I was concerned, was a perfect piece of evidence to the latter theory. I made a quiet note to move Pickman up a notch on my list of "monsters to eliminate." I couldn't say for certain whether Pickman was human or not, or maybe some cross between the two options, but he's an observer, a witness, and the only thing worse than a shapeless beast from another dimension eating humanity is a human who knows of it and encourages its machinations.

The coin grew cold as ice as I brought it into closer proximity with the painting and I almost dropped it as I pressed it to the horrific image. As the coin made contact, the painting flashed brightly. Blinking the flash from my eyes, I noted that the painting was gone and replaced by a large wooden door. With a hard pull on a ring placed in the center of the door, I was able to step into the Miskatonic Armory.

The armory was a thing of beauty. As a historian, I was in love. As a warrior, and I had no doubts that I was a warrior for humanity, I was in lust. The room was more vast than any one room I had ever seen before and I could not see the ceiling. The sheer size of it left me breathless.

The Miskatonic University armory had the traditional weapons as well as the type that I was looking for. Swords, knives, pistols, rifles, whips, cannons, machine guns, weapons you throw, weapons you roll, weapons hidden within weapons, were all alongside torture devices such as iron maidens and racks. While these were all well known and common weapons, I wouldn't doubt that they had to have some sort of special property to be in this specific armory. As I walked slowly among the weapons, I noted that even the sword blades and pistol barrels were all covered with symbols from the dreaded book.

The rows of weapons were blindingly bright, and I meant that almost literally. Most of the weapons had an otherworldly glow about them that radiated not only on the spectra of human sight, but also on the lights between lights. I'm only human, and I couldn't see these colors, but I'd been among the beings of the void enough to sense the disturbance that these colors made. The sense left me with a feeling of unease, but at the same time I knew of the power that this sense implied, and I was in awe of the weapons before me. I'd never been so torn emotionally, or so happy because of the strength of my feelings.

The rows were lengthy, and I never saw the end of one, but I crossed between them and only stopped to inspect the weapons that peaked my interest.

One such stop placed me in front of a large coffin shaped device. If I were a layman, I would assume that it was a large grandfather clock, but I had read of the book and knew it for what it truly was. It was a space craft for traveling in both space and time. It had belonged, allegedly, to a dreamer by the name of Randolph Carter before falling into the hands of Etienne-Laurent de Marigny. Upon a cursory examination of this device, I decided that he must not have liked owning it, as it had a label across it, tied in twine, that read "For Auction." I would have to remind myself to be there for that auction.

Pulling myself from the coffin shaped clock, I turned down another row and was surprised to find that Dean Brandon Smythe was standing there with an unexpected smile on his face.

"You couldn't even trust me to be alone down here, Smythe?"

Smythe kept on smiling and standing there, as if he knew some grand secret that he was more than happy to laud over me. I allowed him this and that was my greatest mistake since getting my cover blown with the Night Watchers.

I'll be the first to admit, I have my faults. I have built a reputation that is mostly of rumors and conjecture, and even this far into my recounting of events, I've nurtured the idea that I'm some sort of magus with large quantities of power at my disposal.

This is the biggest lie of them all. My only powers are the ability and desire to read coupled with a surplus of luck. The ball of flame I conjured in the library had only been a source of light and useless in battle. The telekinetic hold I'd put on the shoggoth had been a spell that anyone could cast who knew the words, and it had only allowed me to immobilize the sun-weakened shoggoth. Also, I've claimed to be able to see everything that others cannot, the lack of sweat on Dr. Stoll, the shoggoth hidden in the room, and pushing my senses outward in the hall. These were not extraordinary powers, but instead only advanced observation skills that I'd picked up in my years of fighting.

I read everything that I come across, no matter how obscure, and I listen to what the peoples of the world tell me. These together leave me prepared for almost anything that the void can throw at me.

All of my explanation is to add credence to the fact that I'm only human, mortal and nothing special, and that is why I fell for the oldest trick in the book.

Shoggoths are shape shifters and illusionists, and without the sun to make a man sweat, there was little I could discover to tell the difference between the former Dr. Stoll and original Dean Brandon Smythe.

Looking back, I should have been able to figure it out by the smile. Even the Dean hadn't shown a smile that creepy in my all too long time having known him.

Oblivious to the surprise that awaited me, I approached the Dean with the full intent of giving him my complete fury at his assumption that I needed a babysitter.

I never made it all the way to him. His arm shot outward, and continued to stretch outward, closing the remaining four foot distance to myself and slamming directly into my chest.

Rocketed back, I slammed into shelving units of blades and guns. The impact sent tingling fire cascading across my back and chest where my sunburned skin was hit. I yelped in pain before finally landing on the ground in a mess of fallen weapons.

I was confused and surprised, but I've never been stupid. I grabbed the nearest weapon to me, which happened to be a non-commissioned officer's sword for the Civil War. Unlike the average style of these types of blades, this blade was black as the very night and reflected no light. Across the blade were symbols I'd seen in several cultures as well as the Necronomicon. I had no idea of the power of this sword, if any, but I wasn't going to let a damned shoggoth stop me from finding out.

I hopped to my feet and sprinted at the monster, who continued to smile as if nothing had happened. At about five feet away I dropped into a slide that, I hoped, left me open for an easy stomping. With effort, a shoggoth was capable of reading a human's mind, yet the heat of battle left no room for that kind of effort. Being a creature of fast movements and incredible strength, the shoggoth's hands shifted into fleshy clubs and slammed down towards my still sliding body.

I'd anticipated this move, as it had been obvious, and slammed my heel into the ground. Using the rest of my forward momentum, I used my foot and my elbow to propel me back towards standing. As I came up and the shoggoth's arms slammed downward, I swung the saber across its chest. It shifted and fell backwards, avoiding the blade and I swung again and again, first an upward slash and another across the chest. Each swing only tasted the dry air of the library as the monster moved with matching speed. My offense wasn't a complete waste though, as it was keeping the monster too busy to retaliate.

Obviously annoyed that this cockroach was trying to bite back, the Dean monster thrust its club arms at my chest again.

Sidestepping the attack only barely, I brought the sword down in a clumsy defense and only managed a small slice of the monster's right arm.

The resulting howl of pain was both verbally abrasive as well as telepathically painful and the shoggoth fell back several steps from the fight. As I stumbled back into solid footing, I watched as the monster's club of an arm smoked and sizzled where the blade had only nicked it. The limb quickly discolored into a brown and grey bruise that stretched up the entire limb. After several more seconds of howling pain, the club of an arm turned to an ooze and then dripped from the monster.

Having lost the troubled limb, the Dean's face then turned to a furious and twisted anger that a normal human face would have been incapable of making. I had a new found faith in my weapon of choice and weaved back into the battle. My faith was quickly lost as the shoggoth's renewed anger battered the weapon from my hand. Before I could retaliate, I was wrapped in the monster's remaining arm, as it slithered from a flesh colored club and into a stretching black tentacle.

Everywhere I was touched by the monster, I erupted in flaming pain, and I was certain that it wasn't all my sunburn. Its presence was acid to my skin, and it wouldn't be long before I'd be feeling my soul leached through that very touch.

The creature writhed as it held me, and I was slammed into more shelves and tables, weapons bouncing across the floor. During this painful period of shoggoth hug, I managed to work my left arm free and found myself once again grasping for the nearest thing that I could find.

As I brought my hand up, I shot the monster between its false eyes and saw absolutely no reaction. The hole the bullet created remained and the shoggoth continued to squeeze me and thrash, causing me to drop the gun, and I worried that I was about to die by shoggoth.

And then the shoggoth shivered. It was subtle, but I could feel it through the monster's burning touch. The shoggoth's image started to slip and it began to return to its normal, oily color. I was dropped, painfully, to the ground and slid back to where the gun had landed. As I saw it, I noticed that it was a simple .38 Smith and Wesson, and was surprisingly loaded. I brought the gun up, but as I did I saw no need to actually pull the trigger.

As the former Dr. Benjamin Stoll struggled to hold itself together, more body parts continued to drip from it. Finally, and with a sudden shudder, the monster collapsed into a puddle.

Keeping just out of distance of the chunk filled goopy remains of the shoggoth, I collapsed as well, hugging the pistol to my chest.

I laid there like that for what seemed like an hour, but was much more likely only a minute or two, when Dean Brandon Smythe stepped into view.

I didn't hesitate as I aimed the pistol right at his head.

The smug bastard smiled a half grin and raised both of his hands. "I heard the alarm go off." He glanced around at the mess that my fight with his pet had caused. "You're the reason we can't have nice things, Dr. Doran."

Taking my gun off Smythe, I stood up and collected the sword from where it had fallen. Grabbing the scabbard, I strapped it to my waist. I would need to get a holster for the pistol, but for now, my waistband would do. I had found my weapons.

"What happened here?" The Dean was no longer attempting humor, and was genuinely concerned as to the mess in his armory.

"Unfortunately," I answered, grabbing a case of .38 ammo from a shelf, "I probably just saved your life."

Chapter 2: The Shadow Over Barcelona

The puddle of shoggoth hadn't finished congealing and Dean Brandon Smythe was already making demands. They all seemed more clinical than anything, demanding that I recount the events of the fight. Did I provoke the shoggoth? Did I inadvertently break the magical leash that Smythe held on it? Wasn't there a better way to go about this than killing his little minion?

The questions came, but no answers did, as I hunted among the shelves and tabletops for a holster. Finally, the Dean threw his hands into the air and said that he'd be in the library when I was ready before storming off toward his secret entrance into this incredibly large armory. It wasn't long after he left that I found my holster. There was nothing special about it, other than being the perfect fit for the gun I had found. On my way towards the very same exit the Dean had used, I grabbed a sack large enough for the two weapons, sword and pistol, and then exited the armory.

I decided to attempt making nice with the Dean long enough to get my ticket overseas, and returned to his library. The Dean was still flustered by what had happened down in the armory and was pacing the room as I entered. I'm sure he was looking for a way to blame me for the battle that had ensued, because to do otherwise would be to admit some sort of fault in himself, and the Dean could never allow that.

Looking inwardly, I was proud of myself. Aside from my recent tussle with the Night Watchers, I had been far removed from any sort of battle for much too long. While I had always prided myself on being an educated man with an outstanding knowledge of cultures across the globe, I could not deny my love for battle. I made no illusions about it. I was a warrior, yet I had gone too long without a fight. I had grown clumsy physically, and my mental discipline was no longer as sharp as I would have liked. I sensed that my world was about to change, and hoped that I would be capable of finding my comfort zone in battle once again.

Seeing me enter, the Dean composed himself as best he could. Much to his credit, he chose to ignore the previous confrontation in the armory and instead spoke directly to the business at hand.

"What are you going to do now?" He prodded.

I was happy for this prodding, as it meant that he was ready to give me whatever I asked for. "I'll need a ticket to Barcelona, Spain."

"A plane ticket?" He asked.

"No. A boat ticket. I don't trust planes." I swung the sack that I'd found down on the nearest table, ignoring the items that rolled out of the way and to the floor.

The Dean grimaced at the mess I was making. He said nothing about it, and thundered on with the details of my mission. "Fine, a boat ticket. I'll have it within the hour." He walked to the other side of the table I was at and faced me. "Why do you want to go to Barcelona?"

I worked at the buckle on the scabbard and slid it off me, wrapping the belt around it. I did my best to hide my annoyance at the Dean's question. An educated man in 1941 should have at least some idea why I would be choosing Barcelona. I chose to placate him.

"Barcelona is the closest city to Nazi controlled territory that I can get to without any sort of notice. When I get to Barcelona, I'll cross the border into France and work my way through and to Germany, before working my way through the final push into Berlin." I slid the scabbard into the sack and then moved my attention to the pistol.

"Alright," the Dean said. "That's logical, but why Berlin?" Much to the Dean's credit, and I'm always hesitant to give him any sort of credit, this was actually a good question. There were a lot of places that the Nazis could have taken the book and they had a lot of reasons not to take it to Berlin, as any would-be rescuers, such as myself, would assume that the book would be taken to the seat of power. The evidence at the Dean's disposal only supported that taking the book to Berlin would not be the wisest course of action. I had more information than he did.

"Oh, it's definitely in Berlin." I pulled the pistol out of my waistband and slid it snugly into the holster. "Berlin is where the Traum Kult resides."

"Traum Kult? I'm not aware of this group." The Dean placed his hands behind his back as I worked at wrapping the belt of the holster around the pistol.

"That's normal. They are Hitler's personal psychic assassins and Berlin is where they are headquartered." I slid the gun into the bag, the handle still readily accessible in its newly wrapped holster, and placed my hands on the table. For the first time since killing the shoggoth, I looked the Dean directly in the eyes. "The word Traumer is German for Dream. Taking the book to the Traum Kult is the only sensible decision. Anyone else in Germany would have no idea how to properly use it and wouldn't be able to do any more damage than a bumbling alumni." I watched his face make no notice of my slight jab and continued. "The Traum Kult would be the only people under the Nazi's control that could access all the book's secrets. If they were so inclined, they could use it to summon the Great Old Ones or possibly command and compel the demons of the void. It's even conceivable that they could use the book to walk the Dream Lands to control, interrogate, or assassinate anyone in the world. The Necronomicon in any of its translations is a tool of incredible power."

"Then why not use their own German version of the book?" The Dean asked.

I couldn't hide my annoyance at this line of questioning. "Use your head. You know why. The English version of the text is the only copy with a complete set of diagrams and schematics for every spell and ritual. That includes all the incantations and blood sports discovered or invented since the German translation had been written. Miskatonic University's copy is a weapon, a gun with extra ammunition, but there's an even better reason to take our copy." I had started orating against my better judgment and took a breath to continue. "At any one time the Traum Kult could use their version of the Necronomicon to walk the Dream Lands and confront American targets. They can use it to kill us, control us, or simply spy on us, but they don't. They don't do this because we would be alerted to this activity within moments, if not before, it was happening. Our own psychics would feel them out and then what would they do?"

I asked him as if I were a teacher asking a child to reason out the obvious answer. In a way I was.

Dean Smythe scowled at me, but took my bait. "Our psychics would alert the appropriate authorities in Miskatonic and we would then use our book to retaliate."

I jabbed my finger at Smythe and said, "Right! By taking our copy of that damned Arab's book, no matter how special it might be, the Führer has severely crippled our defenses."

Smythe's eyes widened in panic. "How long will it take you to get the book back?"

I turned from the Dean, and paced away from him. "As long as it takes." I turned back to him, shoving my hands into my pockets. "Let's get something clear now, before you get any more silly ideas. I do not report to you. Not now and not ever. You are not my boss, foreman, or commanding officer." I pulled a hand from my pocket to jab my finger in his direction once again. "You're an idiot who ignored every warning that you have ever been given and therefore are responsible for the largest mistake since..." I sought for it and found it fairly quickly. "Since trying to compel shoggoths!" I threw both of my hands into the air. "It didn't work for the damned red coats during the Revolution, why the hell would you expect better results. I'll tell you why, because on top of being an idiot, you're arrogant." I allowed myself a breath and returned to the table to grab my bag. "So, no, I will not report to you, and you will have to trust in the fact that I *will* save the world from your ignorance."

The bag packed, I swung the strap over my shoulder with the bag under my arm. The opening was towards the front and I could see the scabbard and the gun inside. I had finished saying anything that I felt needed to be said, and my anger at the man was at its peak. We were done here and I knew that the details of my passage to Spain would be handled by Dean Smythe soon enough. I was ready to leave, and turned to do so.

To my surprise, the Dean grabbed my arm, spinning me back to face him. "We're not done–" he started.

He didn't finish.

My reactions weren't as slow as I'd previously feared. Without remembering making the movement, the pistol was in my hand and pressed to Smythe's forehead.

"Don't push me." I said. "You are a monster and I am no fool. How many bodies have been piling up in the basement of Miskatonic during your tenure?" I was speaking through gritted teeth. I had no idea if I planned to pull the trigger or not. "All that you ever had to do was *hide that damned book.*" I pressed the gun harder into the Dean's forehead. "I've seen it before: you think of the void as a big treasure chest, and, instead of looking inside yourself, you just wait to see what these poor confused students pull out for you to play with. You're addicted to your own morbid curiosity. I. Should. Put. You. Down!" I ended each word of that last bit with a slightly harder push of the pistol.

Smythe's fear was suddenly gone and a small smile showed that he didn't expect me to shoot. "Yes," he said. "I am a monster, but please, tell me how your chosen line of education and heroism is in any way an altruistic act?" He slapped the gun away from his forehead, and I let him. "The difference between you and I, *Dr.* Doran, is that while I was too afraid to peek into the void, you were only too eager."

I put the pistol back into its holster and tightened the bag's draw string. I had no desire to hear any of this, no matter how true it was. In the end my body count wasn't people, it was monsters, and I would be damned if some traitor to his own species was going to lecture me.

The gun secured, I stomped away to the exit of the library. As I grabbed the door, the Dean threw another barb in my direction, and I had to wonder how closely it came to striking home.

"A man like you makes a man like me wonder, Dr. Doran. How much of yourself do you lose every time you take that peek into the void?"

The only communication I received from Dean Brandon Smythe after I stormed out of his office was a messenger that evening. He had come with information on my departure, and no, he was not a compelled evil from the void. Only a young, and perhaps well paid, student. The boat would be leaving early in the next morning and the entire trip would take three days. I was to be riding on a freight barge that would take port in Barcelona. It was exactly what I wanted and I was packed and ready to leave an hour after receiving the departure information. I was packing light and only bringing some clothing and general hygiene needs that managed to fit in my bag with the weapons. I would most likely lose some of the more personal items the closer that I came to Berlin, but the saber and pistol would be in my possession as I confronted the Traum Kult and reclaimed possession of the Necronomicon.

I boarded the freight liner the next morning, before the sun had opened its eyes upon the world. The boat was similar in make to many of the earlier European steam ships, mostly for transporting people and mail, but at about a quarter of the size. It only had one smoke stack and the deck of the boat was about twenty-five feet above the dock. In the morning light, I couldn't see too many details of the ship, but I knew enough to say that the boat looked like the *Titanic*'s orphaned child.

Climbing the steep ramp to the deck, I passed several other passengers. Much in the same way that its much larger compatriots would carry mail as well as passengers, this vessel would be carrying passengers as well as freight. I passed several of them in the dark as I boarded and was unable to see their faces. That didn't stop me from feeling their eyes on me.

I spoke to some of the crew in hopes to find my cabin or where I might be bunking and was soon swept up in the preparation. I spent the next several hours working and laughing with the crew as we moved crates on board and secured them in the hold. It was an hour after the sun had risen before I had found my way to my sleeping quarters.

I found it through horrible directions given to me by my newly discovered friends within the crew. As I entered the small cabin I found bags had already claimed a bed from each of the two bunk beds except for the top bunk on the bed to the right of the door. The bags were not unaccompanied as each of their owners were standing in the tight space. They hadn't been speaking, or at least hadn't been speaking loud enough for me to hear, but they stood closer together than even the tight room required. They had been facing each other, but turned as I stepped in.

As my eyes took in their appearance, I found myself searching my catalog of cultural ethnicities for a definition of what stood before me. They were dressed as port workers in simple wools, yet the odd differences from the average New Englander were all physical. Their mouths were wide, almost twice as much as one would expect, and their eyes seemed equally disproportionate. Large glossy eyes and equally large damp lips did not equal an enormous nose, as each of them had a small, almost nonexistent nose. Two of them wore hats, but their near fraternal similarities allowed me to assume that they all housed large naked craniums.

Each of these exaggerated features were oddities on their own, but they were nowhere near the most inhuman of their characteristics. Their skin itself was the exclamation point in this scene before me. These were pale men. While their clothing assumed a port-like vocation, each of the men lacked any of the sort of pigmentation that long hours in the sun would imply. Added to that fact, their skins were all glistening with a damp look, as though they had some sort of sweaty film covering their bodies. I found myself surprised that they had no sort of overwhelming smell.

I mumbled a quick hello and received no further acknowledgment from them as they returned to their own bunks and sat. The one whose bag was on the other top bunk opted to sit on that bottom bunk with his companion. I threw my bag onto my bunk and turned to eye them all again. They hadn't moved after sitting and now all stared at nothing in particular. It was as if they were waiting for something or had maybe fallen asleep with their eyes open. I was concerned for my next two nights on board the ship.

I gave two more college tries to talking to my new roommates before surrendering to their silence and choosing to explore the boat a little further than my work with the crew had allowed.

While the *Lush Delusion* was small compared to its more famous cousin, the *Titanic*, it was large to my perception. The inside consisted of three cabins for the crew and then two extras for any passengers that might come aboard. That did not include the Captain's small cabin as well. The rest of the ship was deck, engines, and storage.

In this newly christened venture of roommate avoidance, I climbed my way down to the hold. The engines were already spinning with a ferocity and I decided to avoid the heavily (five or more) populated areas for a more peaceful exploration. As the vessel churned against the ocean, the poorly lit hold, with its tied down crates and creaking masses, was incredibly peaceful. For the first time since I'd been discovered by the Night Watchers, I allowed myself to relax.

As I walked, I saw many different types of crates and manufactured goods. At one end of the boat were two very solidly secured cars, and as I moved further from the noisy turbines, I found even more of the larger sized crates, each with a label in a different language.

In my time since leaving Miskatonic University, as a student, I had traveled the world around and seen many such oddities on board craft that, like me, were headed to similarly odd locales. The *Lush Delusion* was no exception. She had many such relics and statues, or so I assumed them to be, as they were each wrapped in the most gentle of ways with straw and newspaper. Only their weird and indecipherable shape gave way to them being anything more than just another piece of machinery. Unlike my previous journeys abroad, I found myself somewhat surprised by the volume of these oddly shaped statues and works of art. While there were hundreds, if not thousands of crates on board, there were at least an equal number of these carefully wrapped statues.

I was examining a large row of these near the front of the ship, when I almost ate a large quantity of bullets.

I had been inspecting the shape of an odd looking statue when I bumped into a large man. There was no give as I bumped into him, and it took me a moment to realize that this was a man at all. Recovering and recognizing him as not being a wall, I at first thought that he was one of my newly discovered roommates. His forehead held the same slant and his skin was glistening as if wet. He also had the large eyes, which still held no real expression. His odd features and lack of personality only supplemented my incorrect assumption that this man had come from my cabin.

He said nothing to me as I regained my composure, but he didn't need to. He held a pistol at my abdomen and in moments after our initial collision, he wasn't alone. Several more of the similar looking folk came to his aid, stepping up behind him with each of their pistols drawn.

I raised both of my palms in defense and stepped back, almost tripping over the statue I had been looking at previously. As I leaned backwards, trying to keep upright, I noticed that the three new men who stood before me were surrounding another of the statues. It stood taller than anything else in the hold of the *Lush Delusion*, and curved with an almost organic look, as though it were about to move, but had frozen in the middle of its movement.

I could sense something in that carefully wrapped package. It was dark and spoke of deep and patient evils. It was hurt, as if shattered. I wasn't supposed to sense that bit, but I'm not your average person. The average person wouldn't have been able to sense the touch of this … thing… The average person would instead feel a shift in their mood towards something darker, something more susceptible to coercion. I, on the other hand, knew it for what it was. It was evil. It was from the void.

I righted myself and looked at each of the men before me. Now everything seemed a little clearer. They were protecting it, and they were not my roommates. That means there were at least seven of this … ethnicity … on board. They seemed to be everywhere and, if the large wrapping in front of me were any indication, they had connections to the darker realms of reality.

My palms were still raised and any peace I'd previously experienced had evaporated. I stepped forward, closer to these people. Without taking my eyes off them, I pointed at their charge and asked, "What's that?" in my most naïve sounding voice.

In a similar fashion to my roommates, they held their tongues and didn't answer. I decided to press my luck and stepped forward, dropping my hands. "My first guess was that it was a statue, but those curves are so organic, so alive." I made to move towards the object for closer inspection and the three large men stepped directly into my path. I stopped and looked the nearest one up and down, as if sizing him up. In reality, I was trying to locate the strong smell of fish that had wafted up my nose upon closer proximity. I sniffed, making no effort to hide my curiosity.

It wasn't his breath.

I sniffed again.

It was him. All of him, and I would lay all bets on his friends having the same putrid smell emanating from them. The smell was so strong. How had I not noticed it until just that moment?

This close, I also took note of the pistol being gently pressed into my ribs. The men spoke no answer to my prodding, but that gun spoke volumes.

I had a sudden and aching wish that I hadn't left my newly acquired pistol on my bunk.

Finally, I decided that I was outgunned and shoved my hands into my trouser pockets. "Well," I said, giving my best *please don't shoot me* smile. "I was only going for a walk. I should get back to it." I fought my better judgment and pulled my eyes away from the larger foreigners and walked away from them. I needed to find out what was going on and who these men were.

I had seen the cabins available, and I walked away with a sincere curiosity: Where would these men be sleeping during our journey? The bunks were all full. All I could assume was some sort of scheduled rotation with shared bunks.

I made my way back to the deck of the boat. The sun shone down on us, unimpeded by clouds. Coming out of the hold, I found myself near the bow of the ship and decided I'd like to see our path behind us and moved myself in that direction. The rail along the path to the back of the boat was set only several feet away from the walls of the main steering room. Without others on the path I could have easily walked along it without being impeded. Unfortunately, the ship was fully crewed, and I walked most of the path hanging partially over the rail, or squeezed tightly against the wall.

It was during this walk, and also during an almost dangerous lean over the edge of the boat, that I overheard the chatter of one of the younger crew. His name escaped me, but I saw that he was talking to a sailor I had met that morning. He was an older man, named James. James was doing his best to ignore the unstoppable flood of verbiage escaping this younger crew member.

"Three, do ya hear me? Three boats this year that have vanished." He had the hint of an accent, but I was unable to place it. Seeing that James had more pressing matters, or that he simply didn't have time for whatever tales the boy was feeling it necessary to share, I grabbed the boy as he began to pass me.

"What three ships vanished?"

He seemed surprised and looked me up and down, before finally settling on not caring who his audience was, as long as they heard what he had to say. "The *Stout Dollar*, the *Hearty Pride*, and the *Hetty*. All of them disappeared in the last year."

I pulled him into a doorway along the wall and we found a little bit of room to breathe. "What's your name?" I asked him.

"Alan, sir. And yourself?"

I decided that this was no place to drop titles. "I'm Andrew Doran. It's a pleasure to meet you, Alan. Could you please tell me about these ships?"

He nodded and continued with his story. "Ships are no longer safe. The first ship, the *Stout Dollar*, crashed ashore a month after its disappearance. All that they found aboard, aside from blood spread across the decks, was the Captain's log. They figure he must have been on the drink, as he wrote that they had been boarded by large fish that started attacking the crew. The log claimed that the fish could be seen trailing them for days." Alan fell into his story and his eyes fell between panic and excitement. "Aside from the blood on the deck, there were no bodies. Not even the Captain." He took a breath, "The *Hearty Pride* vanished soon after that. They found it off the shore about three hundred kilometers and tracked it to where it drifted. They only chanced upon it because of a radio broadcast that went on for seven minutes and thirty-four seconds." He drifted.

"You were there?" I pressed.

He came back to the here and now with a nod. "I kept the stop watch running while another wrote what was said. Most of it was static and we couldn't make it out, but we managed to get one complete sentence." Alan gulped. "There was a scream before we could all hear someone shout 'The fish are killing my men!'"

I grabbed Alan's shoulder and squeezed, trying to lend the man my strength as he relived his nightmares. "And the *Hetty*?"

"The other two boats had their accidents about eight months ago. The *Hetty* had hers about two weeks before we left the port. They found one survivor who managed to steer her in and only barely. They claimed he was mad and threw him into Arkham Asylum, but his story matched the others that had been heard.

"He claimed that the fish had most surely come aboard and that the crew had fought. They fought with all their strength, but for every one fish they killed, two more would climb on board. The fish weren't killing the men, Andrew. This sailor, who only survived by hiding in a food pantry, claimed that the fish were subduing the men and then dragging them over the side and into the depths of the ocean. It was as if they had plans for them."

At his mention of Arkham Asylum, I felt an involuntary shiver course through my body. Arkham is the madhouse for survivors. Any doctor who cherishes his career will tell you about the state of the art facility and practices for treating the mentally ill. They'll tell you that the people who are admitted suffer from a range of mostly diagnosed conditions and that all of them are treatable over time.

What those doctors won't tell you is that Arkham is a house of horrors. Everyone in there has had their psyche broken by the gruesome terrors they've seen. Usually those terrors come from the void and that dreaded book. Of the people in Arkham Asylum who aren't broken and shattered souls, they are monsters. Actual monsters who either possess or copy a being, such as shoggoths, and are captured. Our society has no idea what to do with these beings. They can't kill them, because the world would riot, thinking that society had just killed their beloved teacher, policeman, or postal worker. As an answer, society just locks them away with the same beings whose brains they've already broken.

They say that the doctors who stay at Arkham for more than a year stay forever.

The story of Arkham Asylum is a long and drawn out one, but only a small part of this lad's concerns. These tales of fishmen were not new to me. I have heard of similar rumors in reference to a port town not far from Arkham.

Within the Necronomicon is a large list of monsters and beings from the void that exist and hunt on land. Alongside this list is another large list of monsters that choose to live beneath the sea to hide from our stars. Several millennia ago there was a shift in the stars, and they began emitting something painful to these beasts. To avoid that pain, the creatures hid themselves deep inside our planet and other places beyond our knowledge. One such supposed deity was Dagon, and his presence had last been rumored to surround the port town of Innsmouth. The rumors said that he'd sent his children to the shores of Innsmouth to bring gold to his worshipers as well as to take advantage of the human female form. Dagon was a disgusting creature and he loved the idea of his children being half human.

The Federal Government had received word of these rumors and had acted quickly to quell them the only way that the Government knew how to quell anything: with bombs. In 1928, the entire reef surrounding Innsmouth was bombed and the government was satisfied that it had stopped a possible supernatural incursion.

That of course doesn't mean that Dagon or his ilk were dead. As a matter of fact, I had reason to believe otherwise. Rumors had sprung up all along the east coast claiming that half-men half-fish had been seen dragging women into the waters.

If what this young man had said was to be taken seriously, then these fishmen were now taking it upon themselves to kill sailors for apparently no reason.

I decided to file Alan's information in the back of my mind where I kept most rumors. Rumors were the only means of keeping track of things that people were not willing to admit existed. Myth and stories had become the only reliable source of tracking the kinds of monsters that I make it my business to destroy.

As to collect more evidence for the boy's story, I left Alan to make my way towards the back of the ship. I wished to catch sight of what had caused his fears. The aft of the ship was open and more spacious than the walk to the back had been and I was able to stand without a single soul within arm's reach.

I leaned over the railing and watched the foam that was kicked up by the turbines. I was staring with an intensity that would make most anyone who saw me think that I might have lost something. I had to know if we had those infamous fishmen trailing the *Lush Delusion*. As I peered into the depths of the foam, I ached for my newly acquired pistol to be in my hand.

I saw no fins, gills, or flippers but the foam was thick and the froth could hide the entire Nazi army from any of the best Ally spotters.

A slap on my back made me leap within my skin, and I spun around to confront my attacker. To my continued surprise, this was no attacker, but instead the captain of our fine vessel. I had caught his name from the crew's discussions as I had helped them during preparations.

Captain Ian Drowill smiled and thrust his hand out to me. I took it and allowed him to shake it violently. His grip was strong and he was missing his ring finger on his right hand. He wore a sweater and slacks to complement his Captain's cap.

"Welcome aboard, Mr..."

"Doctor." I answered quickly. "Dr. Andrew Doran. Archaeologist."

The Captain seemed excited about this. "An educated man? We are blessed. What brings you aboard?" His accent had a slight English hint to it. He sounded as though he was from London, proper.

I found myself glancing towards the foam again. "I have work in Barcelona."

The Captain nodded and then did his own glancing back towards the rest of the ship. "Aside from my crew, you must be the only person on board who doesn't look swollen around the head..." He let his thought drift, but I wouldn't let it go.

"Are they of mixed heritage? I can't seem to place their ethnicity." My query snapped Captain Ian's attention back to the here and now.

"What brings you eastward? Just what kind of work do you do, Dr. Doran?" His blatant shift of conversation was a message in and of itself, and I wasn't going to attempt to wrestle the conversation away from his control.

"Politics would be the best description." I answered.

"Trying to enter the war ahead of the rest of your country?"

I smiled genuinely at the Captain. "This trip was more thrust upon me, than of any decision of my own."

"There are easier ways, ya know? Belgium has a legion that doesn't look into people's pasts. What kind of war plan starts in Barcelona?"

"Unfortunately, one that I cannot discuss." I replied.

"Did your government send you?" The Captain continued to pry.

"No," I replied. "A college did." I said it with a finality in my voice that the captain picked up on.

Changing the subject yet again, the Captain became more formal. "The crew and I have our meals away from the ... rest of the passengers. For your comfort, you're more than welcome to join as our guest."

I nodded. "Thank you, Captain. I would greatly appreciate that." I tried one more time. "What exactly is their tale? They haven't been very sociable."

The Captain's attention drifted again as he spoke. "I'm not sure. I've only spoken with one of them, a Mr. Olmstead, and that was only to organize the trip for five of his men. He did not board with them." Captain Ian brought his gaze back to the now and turned it towards me. "From what I have taken to understand, they were forced to relocate after their home had been destroyed in a fire." His face took on a curious look. "They claim to be of Spanish heritage, but I have yet to meet a Spaniard with eyes like that."

"Only the five are on board then?" I asked.

"Olmstead asked for five and five is how many I watched boarding. but I have seen at least eight new faces since then."

"Are you certain?" I pressed.

He hesitated. "Not really, no." He folded his arms. "They are a breed altogether new to me, and I hate to admit that I cannot tell them apart with any sort of ease."

Unfortunately, I knew exactly what the Captain was referring to. I had lived among tribes all over the globe and had never come across a group of people that looked more alike than the few of these 'Spaniards' I had managed to meet.

"What about the wrapped cargo that they have down in the hold? Do you have any idea of what that is?"

The Captain shook his head. "I did not ask. The manifest read only 'building materials.' It is their matter, and I look forward to the day that it is off my boat."

His answer immediately sent a flag up in my mind. His decision to ignore cargo brought aboard his ship was a foreign idea to any captain, and reeked of a psychic defense. I wouldn't doubt that whatever was in the hold had put up a shield to protect itself from prying minds. As my suspicions grew, I became increasingly curious as to what could possibly be going on.

I could see that the Captain was beginning to see my conversation for the interrogation that it really was and I didn't want to see my dinner invitation revoked. I bid him farewell with a firm handshake and worked my way back towards my cabin. I silently hoped that my new roommates wouldn't be there.

I arrived to the first pleasant surprise of the day; my room completely empty. With my roommates absent for at least the next few moments, I took a moment to examine the room. Unfortunately, there wasn't anything to examine. My roommates had only one bag filled with basic clothing. Nothing else marked their existence in this cabin.

Much to my relief, I found my luggage and weapons as I had left them and seemingly untouched. I wondered if this was due to the lack of curiosity in the 'Spaniards' or if the weapons were enchanted. I had heard of some weapons against the void having a similar spell upon them as the package in the hold. I couldn't sense anything on them, but I hadn't been able to get a feeling for their special properties either. I would continue to hope, as such an ability would become useful in Nazi controlled territories.

The dinner hour was coming quickly and I decided that the suspicious nature of my roommates as well as the course of my Miskatonic mission permitted me to carry a weapon at my side. So as not to alarm anyone, I'd bring my sword attached to my belt. It would be dressier than the rest of the crew, but it wouldn't look completely out of place.

Once I was dressed, I made my way to the mess where the crew was mostly there and already preparing to dine. I took a seat next to several of the sailors I had met earlier that day and it didn't take me long to notice that Captain Drowill was missing. I decided to ignore it for the moment and went about making small talk and dining. Amid the conversing, I noted that the food was better than most crew slop I'd experienced and allowed myself to enjoy it.

It wasn't until the middle of dinner that I first sensed the danger that loomed over all attendance.

Previously, I had noted an increased amount of foot traffic coming from above deck and had filed that to the back of my attention. It wasn't until midway through the meal that I realized that the amount of noise above deck did not match with the number of crew that should be above deck. The crew was mostly in the mess with myself, yet it sounded as if double their number was above decks.

As the realization sprung to the forefront of my mind, I stood and shouted, "Where's the Captain?"

Alan, from the tale of fishmen earlier, answered, "The Captain was called to deal with an issue with our guests in the hold."

I did not hesitate. With my current suspicions and the now missing Captain, I expected the worst. "Grab your weapons! We've been boarded."

As the crew stood slowly and began mumbling among themselves, I drew my sword and ran to the door. Turning out of the mess, I could hear the sounds of battle and climbed the stairs two at a time before entering the battle.

The deck was swarmed with what the Captain had called 'Spaniards' and what I could only describe as fishmen. That was what they were, they stood on two legs, but they were definitely born of the void being, Dagon. The handful of crew that had been stationed topside during dinner had dwindled down to only two members and was barely holding the monsters at bay with makeshift weapons. The fishmen were each carrying an oddly shaped blade and were coming from the back of the boat; the wake of the ship.

The Captain was in the hold, as I understood it, and the quickest path to the hold was through the majority of the monsters and towards the aft of the boat.

I was formidable, but this force swarming towards me was more than even I could handle.

I was contemplating the best way to attempt my suicidal run against them when I heard a cry from behind me. From the mess came the crew, all brandishing guns and blades and not hesitating a moment at the sight of the hideous horde.

I had my army and now a chance to make it to the hold.

I leapt forward, sword raised and swung downward hitting the left shoulder of a ducking 'Spaniard' and at least one of my suspicions was confirmed. As my blade cut through clothing and flesh, it also pulled down on the high collar being worn by the man and the last piece of the puzzle fell into place.

The man had gills along his neck.

He was not of Spanish descent. This man was of Innsmouth, and he and his ilk were attempting to set up home in a new port town. Specifically, they were hoping to set up on the Spanish coast.

My sword bit into the monster, body and soul, and black ink seemed to crawl under his skin. His arm, now cleaved from his body, fell to the ground and began to dissolve. This was the product of my sword.

I was the point of the weapon that had become myself and the crew. They fanned out behind me, placing bullets and blades directly into these creatures. Our poorly built phalanx allowed us a slow progression, but progression none the less.

One of the sea devils leapt at me, finned hands splayed and gaping maw prepared to bite me with his three inch teeth. Their advantage was shock and fear, of either I had none. I placed my boot into the midriff of the beast and then brought the pommel of my sword at the base of its skull. The beast fell to the ground and Alan, who was only a pace behind me, placed a bullet into its head.

The next monster lunged at me with their one of their odd blades. I parried two of his jabs before attempting one of my own. The agile creature, avoided my blade completely and gave my leg a slash that burned me, dropping me to my knees. I thrust my sword at his belly, but the beast batted my blade away. I was in deep, and my crew had troubles of their own.

In a last second effort to save my own life, I thrust my palm outward and shouted, "Ia Ia" and a bright light shone from my hand. Most of the creatures from the Necronomicon are nocturnal by nature. They can survive during the day, but are greatly hindered and weakened by the presence of sunlight. In that regard, their eyes are rarely prepared for such a bright flash of energy. Breaking the evening dusk with my finger driven light, everyone on the deck flinched and covered their eyes, giving me just enough time to drive my sword into the abdomen of the fishman. His face immediately started to turn to fluid and I moved onward before seeing the beast puddle on the deck.

I drove my blade into two more heads and knocked my fist into the faces of three more of the monsters before Alan and I had made it to our goal. The door to the hold was unprotected, which concerned me. Obviously, what they held in the hold meant a great deal to these Innsmouth monstrosities and the only door to that point should be securely guarded. This door was not. My concern might have been unnecessary with how many of the fishmen were then occupied with my friends from the crew.

I hesitated only briefly on that thought before rushing through the door and down the stairs with Alan fast on my heels and his pistol at the ready.

As we weaved and circled around cargo tied tightly in place, we did not come across a single fishman or sailor. It wasn't until we reached the oddly shaped cargo that the Captain had hoped to ignore.

His hopes were left unheard. He was on his knees before it, surrounded by fishmen. There was one fishman holding a rifle on the Captain while three others stood surrounding the cargo.

Alan and I slowed our run as this all came into view. We stopped only feet from the Captain, and I kept my sword at the ready while indicating with my free hand that Alan should lower his gun.

"You've lost the battle. Drop your weapons and we'll allow you to leave unmolested."

The fishman holding the Captain hostage smiled, and it was the first expression I had seen in my former roommates. "You lie. We are taking the boat. It is required for our purposes." His voice was accented by a deep gargle, as if he was speaking from underwater.

"I promise you that as long as I'm still standing, you've lost this battle." I waved my sword, indicating the cargo. "If you want that to reach the coast of Spain, we need to open up discussions."

The fishman lost his smile then. "You know what it is?"

"Your little piece of Devil's Reef? Yes, I know what it is and I know who you are. You're survivors from Innsmouth and you're hoping to create a new city for your perverse god, Dagon."

"Hold your tongue, heathen!" The fishman hissed. As he did, he pressed the gun into the Captain's back.

"No!" I shouted, fury filling my every word. "You're murdering innocent men up there. I'll be damned if this continues."

I barked a word that I hoped that they did not know, and with that word I shifted behind the veil. As I've mentioned previously, being behind the veil is not for the light of heart. It suffers no fools and all who enter it are fools. Shoggoths and demons that work for the beasts of the Necronomicon use it to travel long distances, yet I have never known the paths to cut that deeply into the veil. Instead, I was capable of pressing myself into the veil enough to vanish from our reality. The geometry behind the veil is completely alien to me, or any mortal man, and I fought to keep my sanity and move with some control. My goal was not instant teleportation, as that was beyond my power, but to walk unseen across the hold. There are parallels between the dimensions, and I could see the energy that made up the souls of those in the hold. I moved to where I believed the coral from the reef would be based on where the guards had been standing and prepared myself for exiting the veil. My sanity was shredding at the edges, and I started reprimanding myself for such an idiotic ploy. It was during this reprimand that I saw the first of the beings within the veil take notice of me. It moved fast and I only barely found the energy to exit back into my reality before it devoured me.

My ploy, while idiotic in the hazards to my person, had been perfectly executed and I now stood only a foot from the packaged coral.

I pressed my sword against the packaging on the coral and shouted. "Step away from the Captain or my lovely and I will make short work of your cargo."

They didn't react instantly, but when they did they made the right choice. The three guards lowered their weapons and the fishman guarding the Captain pushed him towards Alan.

"Now what?" Asked the fishman.

"First, what did you do with the other ships?"

"The attack on our home lowered our numbers. We took them to procreate and fill our ranks." They'd taken the men for their perverse relations. I almost gagged.

"Now, drop your guns." I demanded.

The fishman who had been guarding the Captain raised his rifle to his shoulder and took aim upon me. "You do not control this situation." He then turned and gunned down Alan.

"No!" I shouted and in that instant dragged my sword up the length of the packaging, severing ropes and paper while also biting into the coral.

As my blade sliced into the coral, a psychic scream was released that penetrated all of my mental defenses and I fell to my knees. All over the ship I could hear as men screamed and roared in pain, but none of the pain from the men matched the screams from the monsters.

They had fallen and now writhed with pain on the floor of the hold. I could hear that it was the same above decks as well. It had only caused me initial pain out of surprise, but had subsided to a dull vibration in the back of my skull. On the other hand, these fishmen were intricately linked with the coral and were disabled by my mild attack.

I pulled my blade away from the coral and watched as the fishmen came back to themselves. "Leave this boat and the men intact and I promise you that we will deliver your cargo for you."

The speaker asked, "How are we to trust you?"

"You can trust in what I know. I know what you are and that if we fail in our promise I know that you will hunt us down. To every last one of us, you will hunt us down." I did know this.

The fishman shook his head. "This relies too much on our trust of you. It is unacceptable."

"The only other option is that I bury my sword into your coral."

The fishman didn't like this. He scooped up his rifle and stomped towards me.

I, like the veil, do not suffer fools.

In one fast movement, I buried my sword into the coral, released it, and stepped to the now fallen and writhing fishman. I then scooped up his rifle, chambered a shell, and shot him in the head. I just as quickly returned to the coral and removed my sword, noting the black veins of destroyed tissue that radiated from where my sword had entered the coral.

I turned towards the remaining fishmen. "He chose not to trust me. My word is my bond and I will deliver this to the coast of Spain." I pointed my sword at the coral again. "Do you trust me?"

They ignored their downed weapons and ran from the hold. I listened as feet across the deck overhead did the same, running for the railing and diving over.

When I was certain that the boat was free of those creatures, I ran to the Captain as he sat with Alan's body.

To my surprise, Alan was alive, albeit unconscious. The bullet had only grazed his skull and the Captain was slapping the boy as I approached.

The Captain noted my approach and nodded towards the coral. "What do we do with that?"

"As I told them, my word is my bond, Captain. When we near the shores of Barcelona we shall push that thing overboard."

"Why not destroy it now?" He begged.

"My words were not bravado. They would know, and they would hunt you down and kill you. Of that I can assure you."

A shiver ran down the Captain's spine. "Fishmen, psychic coral, and a man who can vanish at will… I think that I need a drink, Dr. Doran."

I nodded and smiled. "I think I'll join you after I retrieve my sidearm from my cabin."

Chapter 3: The Whisperers in Andorra

Aside from the failed attempt by the Innsmouth folk to take our boat, my arrival into Barcelona was otherwise unhindered.

I did as promised and, with Captain Drowill's help, released the remains of Devil's Reef into the sea 3 miles off the coast of Spain. While many might see what I've done as helping the monsters, I try to look at it as having saved the lives of an entire ship's crew. It would be against my nature to think otherwise.

Much to my nature's comfort, I might also have made mention to the Captain that our agreement with the displaced fishmen of Innsmouth made no mention of keeping their secret from the local governments.

My movements through Barcelona went unnoticed by any that might have taken interest. I kept my mind and senses open and was left entirely unmolested throughout my brief stay in the beautiful Spanish town. Leaving was the only time that anyone took notice of me in any sense. Along with my ticket for passage, Dean Brandon Smythe had seen fit to give his messenger the proper documentation for when I left Spain. As Spain was my only stop that wasn't polluted by the Nazi influence, it would be the only time that I needed the papers. I presented them to the border patrol and they skimmed over them quickly. Getting out of Spain wasn't a problem, but I was sure that people trying to get into Spain were given a more thorough check.

"Dr. Andrew Doran?" The patrolman asked in heavily accented Spanish. "Doctor of what?"

"Archaeology." I replied and, when I recognized the look he gave me, I added, "I study ancient cultures."

He nodded and skimmed the rest of the document before giving the 'ok' for me to continue.

It was at that moment that I took my first steps into the principality of Andorra.

While I had never set foot in Andorra before this trip, I did know a little about its status in World Politics. Andorra was a neutral state and has done its very best to keep that status through most of the major conflicts. They are most influenced by France and the French Government, but manage to keep distance between themselves and other nations politically. France's interest, as of late, was only military in nature and had become even more so in the wake of the Nazi push into France.

As can be assumed, the idea of a neutral territory so close to Nazi controlled lands caused the Nazi Party concern.

I couldn't figure out why. It wasn't as if devilishly handsome American archaeologists were planning to use Andorra as a stepping point to Berlin…

The biggest difficulty I would have blending in would be Andorra's language. While I'm fluent in most of the romance languages, Catalan is one of the few that I have yet to grasp. Even in the Catalonian city of Barcelona, it was mostly Spanish that I had to contend with. While Catalan is Andorra's national language, the people are also speakers of French and some even speak Spanish. Their French had become increasingly better in the last few years in response to the French Garrison that had taken up residence. Of course, a French Garrison in 1941 was actually a Nazi Garrison, and tensions were running high.

As I had expected, it looked as if Andorra would be my first real attempt at avoiding suspicion.

In the spirit of being completely honest, I was concerned. Hiding among the Night Watchers in Mexico was difficult, but they had been prepared to accept outsiders. If you ignore the fact that they worshiped beings that kidnapped and ate people in their dreams, it wasn't an overly violent situation. Andorra, and every place between it and Berlin, were Nazi lands: lands that were controlled through fear and hiding among terrified people was a dauntingly different prospect.

Nazis or not, my plan wasn't about to change. I still needed to get to Berlin before they used the book.

As luck would have it, I happened upon some interesting news that could facilitate my needs before I had even arrived in Barcelona.

I had been speaking with Captain Ian about my need to get to Berlin. I had done so without explaining the why, yet explained a very vague idea of the path I would be taking. While I didn't explain to him anything about the book or the other monsters I would most definitely be facing, he did not push the issue. I had saved him and his crew and they would blindly follow me to the ends of the earth. It was a touching loyalty, and I felt I owed the man an explanation of my route. It was during this explanation that I mentioned Andorra and how I might enter into Nazi controlled France when we were overheard by the Captain's First Mate, Bruce Tidmore. He stepped in then, and explained that he was friends with a French man who recently escaped France through Andorra. The man had been a pilot for the French Resistance and had suffered a dangerous crash while doing reconnaissance. Barely limping away from the wreckage, the Resistance fortunately found him first and introduced him to an underground movement that ferried Resistance members to safety through Andorra. Mr. Tidmore explained that if the Resistance could get him out, then getting me in should be no problem.

Sadly, that was the entire extent of Bruce Tidmore's knowledge concerning the Resistance. I could find them in Andorra, yet how to find them was up to me. As to how I would do this without giving them or myself away to the French garrison was something I had yet to work out.

Either way, I couldn't do anything until I made it to Andorra's capital city, Andorra la Vella.

That trip took the better part of a day, but after I managed to convince a local farmer to give me a ride in his cart, I made it uneventfully.

Having arrived in Andorra la Vella, I finally had some semblance of a plan. It involved stakeout. I began by wandering aimlessly. It had been a long day and dusk was quickly coming, but I didn't see any reason to slow my progress by getting a room or resting. Anyone in Europe would tell you that resting wasn't going to defeat the Germans.

Wandering through the city had multiple benefits, the first of which was to get the lay of the land. I had never been to Andorra before and getting cornered because I didn't know the streets wasn't an impressive way to go. The other benefit came in learning more about the French Garrison. I used the time to look for the members of the garrison that were floating around. They, unlike the members of the Resistance, had no reason to keep their existence hidden, and made no attempt to do so. They stood out like a shoggoth at a birthday party. The garrison soldiers walked as if they owned the place, and for all I knew they very well might in the next year or more. It seemed that the Nazi party did not know borders and these garrisoned men certainly felt entitled to whatever fear they inspired in the local populace. I watched several displays of it as I wandered the city and saw soldiers rudely bumping shoulders with locals, among other things.

There was one group of three of the soldiers that left a building and were laughing loudly. I followed them at a distance for what seemed almost an hour before I finally discovered the garrison itself. They had done like Nazis and declared an entire hotel for their headquarters. I picked a corner across the street and pretended to be a sleeping vagrant.

The wall I leaned against was a very nice wall and it told me many secrets. One particular secret that it told me was that it wasn't only French Nazis garrisoned in the hotel. There was one very angry German who came and went regularly throughout the time I watched. I took immediate notice of how all the soldiers feared this German. I labeled him a German because he stopped directly in front of me and started shouting at one of the soldiers. The crisp angry tones of the German language could have been heard across the entire city. He was a loud man and loved displaying his authority.

There was a second man that followed close on the German's heels. He was Indian, I believe, and wore a turban around the top of his head. He made no attempt to speak or show any emotion at the German's outbursts. He also wore large thick mittens, which seemed very odd in the almost too warm climate of the season. This sent red flags all throughout my mind and I filed it away to examine at a later time.

It was at this time that I decided to call an end to the evening's surveillance. I took leave of the Nazi Inn and made my way back through Andorra la Vella. My goal was to get as much distance as possible between myself and the garrison. I succeeded doubly by finding a French pub on the far south side of the city. I chose the pub to enable careful questioning about the Resistance and hoped that luck was on my side.

Entering the pub, I was immediately engulfed in smoke and the smell of alcohol. It invaded my every sense, and I found myself craving a large glass of bourbon. Unfortunately, requesting a bourbon in this establishment would certainly grab someone's notice. Instead, I ordered a beer. The glass came within moments of my asking and I paid, but left no tip. I wished to remain anonymous and bourbon and money were not the way to do it.

I had finished most of my beer and seen nothing of suspicious nature throughout the bar before I happened upon my first piece of useful information.

The bartender returned, and in heavily accented French asked me if I would like another drink. I hadn't noticed when he had come around the first time to ask me my order, but he never asked me if I spoke French, he had only assumed. I was suddenly concerned that I wasn't blending in as well as I had been. I let none of this new concern show on my face and nodded an affirmative to the drink.

After he brought me the drink, he began to wipe up a spill from a previous customer who had been sitting near me. As he leaned further over the bar with his rag his long shirt sleeve shifted up his forearm ever so slightly. It was only a fast peek, but it was long enough for me to recognize the tattoo on his wrist.

My personal history in the hands on approach to studying cultures gave me a fair understanding of inking and the symbolism represented within it. As I gazed upon the man's arm, I didn't recognize the symbol from any sort of tattoo-using cultures. Instead, I recognized it from the quarry in my mission. East Indian tribes as well as Native American tribes from the southern half of the United States had used that symbol in their darker rituals. It was a symbol of worship to a perverse and darker god. The Necronomicon referred to it as Yig, the Snake Demon.

Yig was similar to the deity Dagon. They were monsters from the void and had convinced more than a few people to worship them as gods. Both shared a common interest in that they had an unhealthy appetite for becoming romantic with human women.

They wanted offspring. Children gave them the means to work and have a presence in the surface world. The stars had long ago aligned against them and forced them all into exile but the children that the monsters created would act on their parent's call without hesitation.

This bartender had no snake eyed look or skin condition, not like the tribes I'd been in contact with before. I had to assume that he was only a worshiper of Yig and not an offspring. Either way, this was a man who I could force to work with me. I decided that, being my first real lead, I had to attempt to bring him to my aid without scaring him away.

"Gsssash flsaah trisss?" I said under my breath. It meant "What is your nest?" in the language of the children of Yig. If he was of the brotherhood then my words would be more than the mumbling of a drunk foreigner.

His reaction was to stop wiping the bar and eye me. I attempted not to notice and he only continued to stare. It went on like that for a moment before he replied.

"Kassahh, aelem Bissss." *Nest of the Dark Sands.*

I nodded thoughtfully. Or, at least I looked thoughtful. I had never heard of the Nest of the Dark Sands, yet today I could not show a lack of knowledge. I was not Andrew Doran. Today I was a disciple of Yig speaking to a distant cousin.

With his secret suddenly outed, I decided to press my advantage. "Are there many of the Brethren in Andorra?" I asked in French.

He shook his head. "My brethren remain with their nest." He meant some desert or swamp climate. Not Andorra.

"What brought you to Andorra then?"

The bartender shrugged. "I praise Yig, but he does not pay the dues."

I nodded at that and sipped my beer. We spent the next hour discussing the migrations of other followers of Yig, the increased demand for offspring, and the horrible effect of the war on the local economies. I learned that when he wasn't using his name given to him by Yig, the bartender went by Stephan.

"I had to flee my home in Paris just to keep my job." He said when I asked what he did before coming to Andorra.

"Keep your job?" I pressed. "How would the war effect a barkeep?"

His eyes darted across the bar then, scanning for some unseen threat. I knew then that I'd made the right choice in questioning Stephan. He brought his attention back to me once he was satisfied that there was no threat of being overheard. "The Germans are not leaving the brethren alone." "What?" I exclaimed. I was genuinely surprised. What could the Germans want with a bunch of snake worshipers?

He looked at me confused. "How could you not have heard of this, brother? They are adding our families to their ranks." He waved his hands around in a tight circle, not drawing attention but getting his point across. "Not only the brotherhood, either, but also the fellows of Cthulhu and Dagon."

I hushed him then, whispering, "Kta Cthet." *Protect us.*

Brothers of Yig, or any of the followers of void-beings, did not say those names lightly. They believed that saying them would only hurry along the rising of them into our world, and even the followers weren't yet ready for that.

"The brethren, like you and I, are only to shore up their ranks, possibly to add a new element to the war. What the Nazis really want is control over the masters."

I wasn't surprised. This was right in line with them taking the book, but I pressed Stephan anyway. "The Masters?" I begged.

The bartender nodded. "That is what I hear." He shrugged. "They want brothers for their soldiers and shoggoths for their guns."

I laughed, almost too loudly for Stephan's comfort. It was just another group who thought that they could compel shoggoths. It was the same old story to a different tune. Just as quickly as I had laughed, I stopped. I was laughing because the British had tried the same thing with shoggoths during the American Revolution and that didn't go well for them. Entire battalions were consumed by the soul devouring monsters as they turned on those who had summoned them. Just recently, I had even witnessed Dean Brandon Smythe attempting the same damned thing and it had almost ended exactly the same way. He had learned to compel shoggoths from the copy of the book I was currently trying to get into Germany to retrieve. The Dean was only a low-level practitioner. He couldn't fully force his will over the beast and it had broken free.

My laughter had stopped because the Germans now had that very same book, and the Traum Kult were anything but low-level practitioners. As a matter of fact, I was fairly certain that no level yet existed for how well they knew their magics. I was suddenly afraid. If anyone could successfully compel shoggoths it was the Traum Kult.

"Are the brethren doing anything about it?" I asked.

Stephan shrugged. "We hide and help when we can." He thumped his chest. "We are servants only to Yig!"

Help? I thought. *Bingo.*

"How are you helping?" I pressed.

He eyed me then, suspiciously. I was suddenly worried that I had pushed too far. I began to think of what I could say to back pedal when he nodded, deciding to trust me. "I help the French Resistance by giving them a place to meet that is free from Nazis." He nodded again, this time in the direction of a newly filled table.

"French Resistance?" I asked, sounding confused, but knowing full well that I'd hit the jackpot.

"Yes," he scooped up the rag that he had been using and looked from it to me. "If you are looking at staying, I could put you to work in the bar. There are worse places than Andorra for the Brethren."

"Thank you. I will think on it." I was looking again at the resistance members. "Would you mind introducing me to them?"

He shook his head. "I cannot do that. They do not take well to … our kind. I help, but they prefer me helping quietly and from a distance." He frowned.

"Oh, that…" I pulled up my own sleeves, showing my lack of tattoo. "…will not be a problem. I appreciate your help, Stephan."

Before he could pull himself together at the revelation I had just dropped on him, I stepped away from the bar without my drink and approached the table.

Sitting at the table were three people, dressed in the wear of the common folk of Andorra. Two of them were men, one large with suspenders and the other smaller and in a gray cap. The third of their party was a woman.

And a woman she most definitely was, in every sense of the word. Her hair was brown and her eyes were the most beautiful shade of hazel. I was taken by her looks, but even more so by her gaze. I had no doubt that the gaze she held had commanded armies. I ignored the two men and walked directly to the real power at the table.

I thrust my hand toward her, "My name is Dr. Andrew Doran, and I'm an—"

"American." She interrupted me with a thick French accent. "Yes, you are an American, and you know who *we* are." It wasn't a question and she eyed the bartender angrily.

Suddenly, I noticed that she was aiming a gun at me that I hadn't seen her drawn, and I had been watching.

Closely.

I raised both of my hands slowly and set my bag on the floor. "I'm not a threat. Actually, I need your help." I pointed at the gun. "Why don't you put the gun down and hear what I have to say?"

She rested the gun on the table but didn't take her hand off it.

"Much better," I said, smiling. "I'm going to try this again." I stuck out my hand slowly this time. "I'm Dr. Andrew Doran. I'm an archaeologist."

"And why do you need our help?"

"Have you ever heard of Miskatonic University?" I was taking a shot in the dark, but with a brother of Yig only ten feet away, I assumed that it wasn't a completely blind shot.

I hadn't completed saying "University," when her eyes revealed to me that she knew of the place. "The Nazis took the Necronomicon. I have the knowledge and ability to get it back, but I need to get into France. That is something that I can't do without your help."

She didn't move, but I could sense the emotions pouring off her. She was conflicted with anger and some sort of low level fear. Both were more than justified. I was demanding aid and had shown her a possible threat.

The smaller of the men at the table, the one in the hat and with a mustache that was almost as thick as mine, spoke up. "We only get people out of France. We are not in the business of getting people into France."

The bigger man added, "The Germans would take notice of us."

I remained quiet. It wasn't to my benefit to speak with them. The decision was resting in the lovely woman's hands.

The French goddess across from them eyed her gun again before looking at the hatted man. "We have to help him."

He began to open his mouth, but stopped at her look. "Without our help, the war is lost." She said, plainly. "No," she sighed. "The entire world would be lost."

As the night went on, we sat there at the table and discussed what exactly it was that I needed.

Once a week, a large truck would arrive with supplies for the city taverns. There was a winery near the eastern border of Andorra that would deliver crates of wine to the various taverns throughout Andorra. Several of those taverns were in Andorra la Vella. In each of those trucks were also workers for unloading the alcohol. Those workers were actually downed pilots of the French Resistance. At each tavern one or two of the workers would unload the crates, and none of them would get back onto the truck.

Except this time.

My benefactors were quick to introduce themselves after I gave my complete story and showed the magical weapons in my bag for proof of my validity. The man in the cap was Felix. He was an alternating truck driver and claimed that, before the war, he had owned the greatest winery in Andorra. His large friend was Robert. Robert didn't speak much, he seemed more content to drink whatever Felix ordered for him and keep to himself. The little bit of dialog that I did gleam from the giant led me to believe that he had been part of the French military before the Nazi move into France. Some point after the invasion he was injured and joined up with the invasion. While he didn't elaborate on his injury, I noticed a limp in his step when he stood to collect drinks from Stephan.

My angel and savior for the evening was the beautiful Olivia. She was hell-bent on keeping it strictly business, so I didn't get much about her background other than what my observation could detect.

Even with my keen observation skills, I was left with little information. I knew that she carried two knives on her: one at the base of her back (I noticed from the angle at which she sat) and the other tucked inside her boot. The one in her boot I noticed only because of the bulge it produced. By the way she held herself she was either military trained or had seen much combat since her joining with the Resistance.

The other thing that I noticed, and was pleased to do so, was that she was also noticing me. Her eyes had examined my own boots and my bag before taking a seriously detailed path up the entire length of my body.

I wish that I could have found it flattering, but I had already pegged her as a combatant. She was conducting the same analysis as I had.

It was her idea to have me ride with the trucks on the return.

The reason that the trucks worked so well for shuttling the pilots out of France was because of the wine. Nothing worked quite as well for a bribe as a truck full of wine. For this same reason, the return trip, which was what I planned on taking, would be difficult because all the wine would have been delivered.

I asked only once if we could keep some of the wine on the truck, just in case, and she made it very clear that we could not. Almost violently, she said, "I will not risk the lives of French heroes for any American. Not even one with a mission as vital as yours. You will deal with Nazi entanglements yourself." I thought her scolding done but then she raised her hand, jabbing her finger at me. "If we get discovered, you will have worse to deal with than Nazis, I promise you."

"We?" I demanded. "I'm sorry, sweetheart, but this isn't a caravan." I crossed my arms. "The more of us in the truck, the more they will notice us."

Felix shook his head. "No, Olivia must come. We will need her to speak for us. The Nazis do not control Andorra, but no one polices the roads. If we get caught on the roads, Olivia might be our only salvation." "Why's that?"

"I own the winery that delivers to Andorra la Vella." Olivia answered.

I calmed myself down and apologized for my outburst. "When do we leave?" I asked.

Olivia stood, "We go now."

I was surprised. "Now?" I had not expected them to be ready so quickly. "It's late in the evening. They will know something is up."

She slammed her hands down on the table. "Listen, American. Every second we delay is another second that the Germans hold on

to your book. There is only one threat at this time of night, and that
is the garrison on the Eastern side of the city. Once we get past that,
it should be simple to get you into France."

I decided that angering this goddess any further was something
that would not bring me benefit and I stood. Shouldering my bag, I
bowed and waved her toward the door. "After you, Madame." She
cast me a glare and walked past me at a clipped pace.

Felix laughed but I earned a very hard stare from Robert. I
straightened when I noticed his look and left the bar on the heels
of Olivia and Felix, leaving Robert to follow and stare at the back of
my head.

The truck was a simple shipping truck. Robert and I sat in the
opened back where the wine would usually rest, while Olivia rode
shotgun to Felix driving.

Crossing Andorra la Vella on foot had taken me about an hour,
but in the truck we made the same journey in a quarter of the time.
We slowed as we came to the garrison. Soldiers were standing all
over the road between the old hotel and where I had observed them
from across the street previously.

Much to my surprise, the garrison soldiers mostly ignored us.
They glanced at the truck, but felt no need to approach it.

This was what I had thought, anyway. Then I saw the fellow
with the turban and mittens. As his cold eyes met mine, I felt him
lash out at me with his mind. I was unprepared and couldn't bring
my defenses up in time. I knew then that we had been caught. He
had sensed something from me, as I too had sensed that he had
something different about him. It was subtle at first. I felt as though
I was looking at a man, but it was a man in a shell. He wasn't quite
himself. I was confused by this, but had no time to investigate it. As
soon as I sensed his *difference,* his own senses alerted him to myself.
He raised his mittened hands and shouted something that I was too
far away to hear.

Unfortunately, the soldiers near to me were not too far away to
hear it. Their guns shot up toward us and they began to bark that
we stop. Before Felix had full stopped the truck, Olivia was violently
pulled from it and soon joined by the rest of us.

As we were on our knees beside the truck, guns aimed at us, the
Indian in mittens stepped up to us and eyed me specifically.

"You are seeking the book."

It wasn't a question, but I answered anyway. "If you could please direct me to the library, my friends and I seem to have gotten lost." I spoke in English.

He answered me in English as well. "You must be Dr. Doran." He touched my face with his mittened hand, and what I felt underneath were not fingers. "I was warned that you might be gracing us with your presence."

"Oh?" I asked. "Did my agent call ahead? I wasn't supposed to be booking shows this week."

"Your laughter hides your fear, Doctor. You know that I have the ability to make your life hell."

In all seriousness, I answered. "I've been to hell, asshole. Do your worst."

He backhanded me then and I blacked out.

I awoke in a dimly lit hotel room. The bed and dresser had been removed and I sat on the floor. I was the only occupant and I had no idea where they had taken Olivia, Felix, or Robert. My hands were bound behind me and I was tied to the radiator. I couldn't see my bag anywhere, but I decided to push that concern aside for the moment.

I knew spells that might break my bindings, but they involved fire and being able to see my target. I wasn't going to blindly shoot flame at my wrists unless I ran out of other options.

Twisting my binds against the radiator, I tested their strength and quickly decided that I had been tied by professionals. I wasn't going to be muscling my way out anytime soon.

Fortunately, I didn't have to worry about muscling out of anything. The door to my room flew open and two large Nazi soldiers came in while a third trained a gun on me. They untied me from the radiator and then rebound my wrists before dragging me out of the room and down the hall.

We didn't go far before they pushed open another hotel room door and dragged me in there. There were three chairs set next to each other and facing the window. Two of them were occupied. The soldiers pushed me hard into the chair furthest to the right and tied my wrists to it. To my left sat Felix and then Olivia. Standing in front of us was the German I had seen barking orders out in front of the hotel earlier that day.

I looked across Felix to Olivia and smiled. "Did you guys bring any snacks? I like to munch during the show."

Before I could witness the scowl that I am certain I had earned from Olivia, the German's fist flew out and broke my nose.

"That will be quite enough of your mouth. Dr. Doran." His clipped German accent was destroying the beautiful French language. "Now, I know why you're here. Looking for your book, I assume, but who are your friends?"

I shook the stars from my vision and ignored the blood cascading over my mouth. "Well, the lovely lady is my sister, Janet, and the gentleman is her soon-to-be husband. I'm taking them on a tour of Andorra for a wedding present!"

I took another punch to the face and this time it was in the eye. Hans Punchy knelt in front of me then, "Are they part of the Resistance? Do they know about the book? Are you an American spy or are you just stupid?"

I lost most of my sharp tongue at that point and settled for the witty retort of a blood filled spit into his face.

Wiping the spit, he drew his pistol and aimed it at Felix's head. "What is your name?"

Felix said nothing and only stared at the German.

The Nazi dropped the aim of gun to Felix's leg and pulled the trigger. The resulting noise of the gun left my ears ringing, but as the ringing died down I could hear Felix howling in pain.

"It is a simple question," the bastard German said. He pointed at himself. "Watch how I do it. I am Lukas Herrmann," he pointed back at Felix. "And who are you?"

Felix swore loudly in French before shouting, "To Hell with you!"

Herrmann stared at Felix for what seemed like forever. Finally, he turned to the far wall and shouted, "Edward! Bring it in!"

The door creaked open and the Indian with the mittens came in pushing a cart with a large cloth covering something underneath it.

Edward, the Indian with the oddly un-Indian name, brought the cart to a rest directly before us and then tore the sheet off the top.

It took me a minute to comprehend what I was looking at, but once I understood what was before us, I knew, without a doubt, the depth of the evil forces that had coalesced in Andorra la Vella.

The cart was covered in a menagerie of machinery, most of which was too alien for me to recognize. The two simplest pieces were a large piece of glass with cables running from it and a jar that housed a human brain floating in some liquid. I held no reservations that this was definitely a human brain. It was the Nazis: *of course* it was a human brain.

Edward straightened and slowly pulled off one of his mittens. As he did, all of my theories were confirmed. Underneath his beautifully knit mittens were pincers. They were a luminescent shade of blue. He was insectoid in origin, and I'm certain that if he were to take off the rest of his disguise, we would all see him for the large Mi-Go that he was.

Mi-Go were an exploratory species of alien from the far reaches of the galaxy. Some suspected that they weren't even from our time, having instead traveled across space and time to avoid their own extinction. When they were on Earth, they loved to plague rural communities, and their ghastly frames had turned them into creatures of myth and scary stories. They had many advanced technologies and prided themselves on gathering knowledge from the species they encountered. One such piece of technology was sitting before us then.

Using his pincer hand, Edward the Mi-Go reached down to the series of dials on the base of the jar and turned one of them.

The result was a flicker in the upright piece of glass. The flicker began to coalesce and focus and it wasn't long before an image began to form on it. It was as if a signal were coming from far away and only time would bring it into focus.

The image began to take on a very specific shape and, to our horror, we recognized it.

It was the unconscious face of Robert. Reaching down to the dials again, Edward hit a small switch and we watched in terror as Robert's eyes flickered to life, and our friend awoke.

"Where…" His voice began from a speaker, but it was distant, and his mind must have had to reach across the same distance that his face had, because his words were slow to come. "Where … where … am I?"

Felix was the first of us to say anything. "Robert! Robert! What have they done to you?"

Robert turned his eyes toward Felix and smiled. "My friend." He said in his deep French accent. "I worried that I would never see you again." He frowned and his brow furrowed. "I was being tortured. I saw things … the Indian, he isn't what he seems." Felix was speechless again, but he nodded. "They did horrible things to me, Felix. I was certain that I was dead."

I hadn't ever seen this horror perpetrated by the Mi-Go before, but I had read a paper describing it in detail. Knowledge truly is power, and my knowledge of this contraption helped me to dispel the shock at what I was seeing much faster than either Olivia or Felix. Broken nose or not, my wits were finally coming back to me.

"You are dead, Robert." The Mi-Go looked at me then. "This monster cut out your brain and dropped it into a jar. From there they can force you to tell them anything they want to know." I turned my eyes to Herrmann. "Which leads me to wonder why we're being asked any damned questions at all."

Herrmann shrugged, "He only knows so much." He knelt before me again. "I am going to systematically destroy your companions and I am going to make you watch. I want you to be mine, Dr. Doran. The Traum Kult has spoken highly of your interests, and I believe that they would reward me well if I could give them the tamed and broken Dr. Andrew Doran." He smiled then and it was a wholly evil thing.

"Your allies' lives mean nothing to me, but something to you. Even though you just met them, I can tell that you're a man who values life. I can see it in your eyes as you look at what has befallen your companion." His hand brushed the jar. "So, to begin breaking you, I'm going to make you watch as *my* friend slowly gathers the minds of your friends for his collection."

Edward reached forward then and turned another dial on the base of the jar. The static energy in the room increased suddenly and we were all subject to Robert's screams as intense pain was sent directly into his brain. Felix began to shout and beg for them to stop hurting his friend.

From the table, Edward grabbed a tool with his unmittened pincer. It was an instrument with an oddly shaped blade, similar to a scalpel, but I had never seen its like before. He stepped up to Felix and pulled his head closer with his hand that still wore the mitten. Olivia remained quiet, but her eyes filled with tears then.

The first thing that Edward did was stab the blade of the odd tool into Felix's throat. The poor driver choked slowly on his own blood. I struggled against my bonds and watched as the Mi-Go began cutting into Felix's scalp before he had completely expired.

Herrmann must have had some sort of warning from the Traum Kult about my history, because my struggling against my ties caused him to punch me, yet again, in the face. I spat blood onto the floor and then gathered my will. Felix was the last, I would not let another die.

I shouted the spell that I had been so hesitant to shout earlier and tried not to think on the repercussions of not seeing my target. I had committed to saving at least Olivia's life.

"Fthalan!" I screamed and released a flood of will out through my hands.

Excruciating pain flared in my hands and seared through my flesh. As I howled in pain, my wrists came free. My hands were still on fire and I thrust my right forward in a fist, hitting the Mi-Go square in the false face. He fell, and I watched as his fleshy mask slid sideways on his face. As he fell away from Felix's corpse, I threw my other flaming hand out and grabbed at the oddly shaped tool.

That was my big power play and I was one holler away from being shot by the guards just outside the room.

I kicked hard at Herrmann, thrusting my boot deep into his abdomen as he moved to bring his pistol back up.

The flame on my hands was starting to die down when a new idea suddenly came to me. Shouting "Fthalan," again, I took aim this time and turned the door into a wall of wood and fire. It would not halt the guards, but hopefully it would slow them down.

The Mi-Go was recovering and leapt at me with his human mask still sliding from its proper placement. His crooked face was where I aimed when I sidestepped his leap and punched out. He fell down onto Herrmann, stopping him again from bringing his gun forward.

No sooner had they collided that I dove on top of them, stabbing at the Mi-Go with his own instrument. As I stabbed down with one hand, my other hand grappled to take away Herrmann's pistol. I barely succeeded and jumped up and off them.

As they lay there, the fight suddenly gone from both of them, I looked over at what remained of Robert. I kept the gun on the two on the floor as I stepped closer to Robert and flipped the same switch that had caused him to scream.

As the pain went away, Robert looked up at me. "I'm sorry, Robert." I said. "Please, forgive me." I then pulled the gun away from the two and put a bullet into the brain that was Robert. His image froze on the screen, but there was nothing left behind his eyes. Robert was gone.

The guards increased their efforts with the door, and the wall of flame didn't stop them from kicking it. It wouldn't be long before they were in, and I was going to need help.

I went to the back of Olivia's chair and carefully cut her binds with the Mi-Go's blade while keeping the gun trained on Herrmann and his monster.

"Do you know where my weapons are?" I asked her.

She nodded. "They were in the room I was being held in. Two doors," she pointed at the wall, "that way." She stared at my still smoking hands. "Can you do … that thing again? But to the walls?"

I shook my head. "My magical talent is severely limited. I run out of juice very quickly." It was the truth, I was already feeling very tired from the two bursts of fire I had created. My real power came in hand to hand combat, not magic.

"Well, American. We are surrounded by Nazis and only have one pistol. Would you care to show me an American solution?"

"With pleasure," I answered, but I had no immediate idea what I was going to do.

Then, my eyes falling on Herrmann, I had the beginnings of an idea.

Stepping up to Edward the Mi-Go, I placed two bullets into his head. "That is for Felix and Robert." I put a third bullet into his abdomen. "That's for the rest of humanity." Then I grabbed Herrmann by the collar and pushed him in front of me, turning him so that he faced the door.

It was only barely in time that I did this. The flaming door burst open at that moment and, as the guards filed in, Olivia jumped behind me and my German shield.

In French I shouted, "Back! Get back or Herrmann joins the Mi-Go!" The Nazis must not have been well treated by their German superior. They hesitated to move for a split second more than I expected. Finally, guns still raised, they slid to the left side of the door. Olivia, Herrmann, and I moved slowly, but already I could hear the soldiers throughout the rest of the makeshift garrison stomping their way down the hall.

I leaned out into the hall with my reluctant companion and Olivia. One end of the hall had marching soldiers with weapons raised. They came to a halt as they saw us. The other end of the hall was empty as far as I could see.

Without looking at Olivia, I asked, "Which way to the room that you were in?"

She pointed. "Two doors." To my relief she pointed in the direction away from the enemy. We slowly started backing into the direction that she indicated.

"Watch our backs," I told her. It would do me no good to keep the Nazis at to our front if another group of them were to arrive behind us.

To our fortune, none did. In what seemed like an eternity, we were finally at the door.

"Open it!" I demanded of Olivia. She quickly did and we slid inside. The Nazi army was slowly creeping toward us and we moved further into the room.

"If anyone comes into this room," I shouted, "we will kill the German!"

I slammed the door shut and threw Lukas Herrmann to the floor.

Before he had even hit, I tossed his gun to Olivia. "Keep an eye on him. If he moves, shoot him." I then ran across the room, scanning for my bag. I found it finally in the bathtub in the bathroom.

It was too much. The bag had clothing, my guns, my diary, and my transit papers. They were too much to attempt to get out of the hotel with and would only slow us down.

My plan was to get out of the hotel. Easy to say, but difficult to execute. We were in neutral Andorra, but the hotel might as well have been Berlin. Once we were out of the hotel the heat would die down considerably. It was just a matter of orchestrating how we would get out.

I dumped my bag and began rummaging through it. I slid my diary into my belt at the base of my back and then tucked my shirt in around it. Then I kicked the clothing aside and pocketed the pistol ammo as best I could. I then belted on the holster and attached the scabbard to my belt. The transit paperwork would be useless from here on out. My gun would be my passport.

Finally ready to take on whatever the Nazis would throw at me, I turned toward Olivia. She was sniffing the air. Out of curiosity I did the same.

Smoke.

I was confused at first and then it hit me and I smiled.

"It would seem that our Nazi friends are losing the battle with the fire I set." I took a deep breath, "Maybe I have one more in me." I began to gather my already too taxed will in preparation of another fire. A touch from Olivia stopped me.

Keeping her gun on Herrmann, she walked over to where I had kicked my clothes, and kicked them over. Underneath them was a book of matches that must have fallen from my bag. For once, luck was with us.

"Save your strength," she said, and quickly set to lighting the curtains on fire while I kept my gun trained on Herrmann.

When the curtains caught fire I moved to the door and peeked into the hall. It was filling thickly with black smoke and I could only barely make out the Nazis.

Scooping up Herrmann by the collar, I stomped out into the hall with no warning to Olivia. She caught on and I could hear her step behind me quickly.

We ran toward the soldiers, I thrust Hermann forward and placed my foot in the center of his back. My following kick sent him sprawling into the soldiers and I began firing with my pistol. It was only a six shot .38, but my aim was true. I missed only once and five of the soldiers went down in the tight space of the hall.

Battle was nothing new to Olivia and the French goddess stepped forward as I reloaded. I watched as she fired and she placed many well aimed shots into the mass of Nazis.

This was a scare tactic, and we were not going to be cutting our way through this battalion before us. The narrow hall gave us a slight advantage, but we had no cover and would soon be overwhelmed.

Olivia kept firing until I shouted, "Down!" I took over firing as she ducked and slid in behind me. Backward was our goal, to the empty end of the hall.

At some point previously, Olivia must have taken ammo from Lukas. She knelt behind me reloading while I fired at any head that threatened to poke out of the Nazi crowd. She reloaded twice during our move back towards the bend in the hall. Using their own men as cover, it was as we approached that bend that the soldiers had finally found their footing and began returning heavy fire. Over the smoke and gunfire, I could hear Herrmann shouting in both German and French, demanding that they kill us.

We finally rounded the corner in the hall, and an idea came to me. I pointed at a painting on the wall, and shouted to Olivia, "I'll cover you!" She understood my meaning and began setting the painting on fire. I fired into the plumes of smoke billowing into the hall. As the painting went up in bright orange curls of flame, Olivia took it down and slid it across the floor and against a far wall. The flames leapt upwards and caught the dry wallpaper very quickly.

We sprinted down the hall away from the Nazis and fire. The stairs came at us quickly and we took them two and three at a time. We were on the third floor and terrified that we were about to run into more soldiers, but they must have all been upstairs.

We came to the first floor and we had not seen a single Nazi, yet. It was in the hotel lobby that we found that some soldiers had been left to guard the front.

Our emergence from the stairs took them by surprise and, placing several bullets into one soldier, I took the time to draw my magical sword. I dropped it onto the arm of the nearest Nazi as he drew his pistol and I wasn't surprised that it did nothing except remove his hand at the wrist. Its magical properties, as I had assumed, were only effective against beings of the void, but its sharp blade was effective against whatever I introduced it to.

Olivia made short work of two more of the soldiers as I shot one and stabbed at another. As he rested on my blade, abdomen pierced by black metal, he still raised his weapon, intent on taking me with him. I swung my pistol around and shot at his head. To my dismay, my gun only clicked on an empty chamber.

I had no time to think as terror filled my mind. His gun took aim and he pulled on the trigger, but I was fortunate to not be traveling alone. Olivia's gun fired a second before his could and his head blossomed in an explosion of gore.

I pulled my sword free and we exited the now empty lobby into the street.

Running across the street and away from the flaming hotel, gunfire echoed behind us. The pavement at our feet shot upward in chunks as Nazis came from the blazing hotel, hell-bent on finishing us. Already Andorran Police were driving up and jumping from their cars.

Our truck was where they had left it and we reached it only barely as gunfire grew closer and closer to us.

Andorran Police knew this was Nazi business and must have feared retaliation. They made no move to stop us or to help the garrison. It would seem that they had only come to watch the old hotel burn to the ground.

I hopped into the truck on the passenger side and slid over to the driver's side. Turning the key, the engine roared to life. Olivia jumped in right behind me and slammed the door shut. I gunned the motor then, and took off in the direction of the Andorran/French border.

Ten miles had passed before I slammed on the brakes and took my first calm breath. My heart was still racing and I looked at Olivia; terror and soot covered her face.

"I think that it would be best if you got out now." I said. "Thank you for your help. I'm sorry about what happened with Robert and Felix. The Nazis will be expecting me at the border, and they won't be nice to anyone traveling with me."

She gave me a look so hard that I feared she had been turned to stone.

"Americans!" She exclaimed. "I said before that you're not getting through the border without my help. I am going with you."

I jabbed my finger in her direction. "No," I said, anger rising in my voice. "No more help from you. I appreciate what you've done, but you can't go with me. That's final!"

"Final? The man driving my truck is trying to tell me what is final?" She crossed her arms. "I go with you. There is no other option. If you happened to notice, the Germans were also shooting at me. I am no longer safe in Andorra. You need me to get you into France and you could use someone to watch your back."

I faced forward and tried to clear my mind. She had a point. We had worked well together in the hotel, and the Germans would certainly be hunting her in Andorra la Vella, but if she were to come with me it would be another weapon that the Nazis could use against me. Also, I didn't want to get wrapped up in her war. The war wasn't my concern. My concern was getting the book back. Olivia had made no attempts to hide her goals of helping the Resistance. She could be easily distracted from my quest.

My decision was made when it crossed my mind that making my way through a Nazi controlled France was going to be tough. I was worried that she would use me to help her and the Resistance, but that was when it crossed my mind to instead use her and her connections.

The devil be in me, but I would not pass up any sort of militant help that might ease my journey into Berlin.

It also hadn't escaped my notice that Olivia hadn't flinched at the mention of Miskatonic or my use of magic.

"Alright. You can come, but my goal doesn't change. We need to get the book back. If I think you are slowing me down at all, I'm cutting you loose."

"Oh, Dr. Doran, I promise you, I will not be the one slowing you down. You'll have to work hard to keep up with me."

I smiled and raised my eyebrow, "Oh? I like the sound of that."

Olivia rolled her eyes at me. "Keep it in your pants, American. You are not my type."

I smiled and started the truck back up. Putting it into gear, I replied, "Yes, ma'am," and took off for the northwestern border of Andorra.

Chapter 4: The Thing in Lyon

Olivia had been correct.

I needed her more than I had expected.

Her truck wasn't the only reason, either. I needed her papers. Olivia had papers that allowed her to continue carrying her wine across the border to Andorra under the condition that she took a shipment to the French Garrison as well. When she explained these papers to me, Olivia expressed the belief that as the war escalated, those papers wouldn't hold any importance anymore. We were fortunate that they still worked for us.

It also helped, sadly, that Felix could not make the trip across the border with us. The Nazi soldiers had expected a driver and they would have been hesitant to believe that Olivia would have been hired on for the job.

We were only stopped once more after the border crossing and that was when the real fear sank into my soul. They began demanding that we explain what our business had been in Andorra and immediately began questioning any ties that we might have had with the French Resistance. It was obvious that our rendezvous with the French Garrison had been spreading quickly.

When they then demanded our business in France they ignored Olivia while she attempted to explain and instead barked that they wanted the explanation from myself.

I gave Olivia a quick glance, but then summoned up my will and put every ounce of effort into my French accent.

"My name is Felix Laurent. We were returning to Martin Fayette's winery, on the eastern side of Lyon." It seemed to work that I had used Felix's name. It would have done me no good to use my own. If anything could have been learned from our run in with Lukas Herrmann, it was that the Germans had a good idea of who

Dr. Andrew Doran was and what he was aiming to reclaim.

The soldier eyed me with a look I couldn't quite read and then continued. "And who do you work for?" I had to tread carefully here. My lies were only getting deeper, but I had to stick with the story that Olivia had shared with me.

"As I said, I work for Mademoiselle Olivia's father, Martin Fayette. I drive the truck." I nodded to first Olivia and then the truck that was directly behind us.

He nodded as well, ignoring the truck and instead indicating Olivia. "This is Mademoiselle Olivia Fayette?"

"Yes," I said.

"Why is the daughter of your employer riding with you?" His suspicions were growing.

I shrugged while keeping my hands above my head. "When she asked, I said yes. How could I deny such a..." I only hesitated because I couldn't remember the French words. The hesitation actually worked to my advantage, as the soldier holding the papers caught it and thought that I was hinting at indiscretions.

He snickered and glanced at Olivia inappropriately. I was surprised by the sudden heat I felt rise in my chest. My warrior lust was rising because of this man's glance at Olivia. I kept my ridiculously misplaced jealousy in check and gave a knowing smile when he looked back at me.

The Nazi soldier handed Olivia back her work papers and allowed us to get back into the truck. After we did, we began prepping a new plan.

The further from Andorra we were to travel, the less believable our story was going to be. Our new plan was to sell the truck in Lyon.

Lyon was a large city. It wasn't quite Paris, but it wasn't Andorra la Vella either. According to Olivia, our largest issue would be the same as our issue in Andorra: a large number of Nazi soldiers.

We hoped that if we kept our wine story, adding the fact that the war had butchered profits and we needed to sell the truck, we would escape Lyon relatively unscathed.

As the truck pulled away from the soldiers Olivia looked at me, her face was more unreadable than usual. "You did well back there."

I smiled, more from shock and confusion than anything else.

"Thank you. For a second there, I was worried we'd have to kill them all."

That earned a smile from Olivia. "Well, I would have," she said. "I'm sure they would have shot you as soon as they realized that you were an American."

"Yes," I replied. "I'm sure they have as much faith in Americans as you do."

Olivia patted my knee then. I'd be lying if I didn't say that her touch gave me the good kind of chills. "You're improving my opinion of your people every day. By tomorrow, I might even stop cringing at the sight of you."

I laughed. "That'll be the day."

Driving into Lyon was surprisingly simpler than driving to Lyon had been. We entered the city at around five in the evening, local time. We had the truck sold by six.

In my honest opinion, Olivia had been ripped off. My opinion didn't matter in the Führer's France. Olivia had explained that if you were selling a truck in this poor economy than you were more than likely running from persecution and any price would be better than keeping the truck. We had been lucky to leave with even a somewhat decent price.

We took a quick dinner at a café near to where we sold the truck and we didn't speak. Olivia had been keeping her eyes on the people. She was looking for someone. It wasn't just soldiers either. I was keeping my eyes open for them and Olivia's eyes never crossed any of my potential threats.

We'd been walking for about ten minutes after leaving the café before I realized that Olivia must have found what she was looking for. We were following someone.

My French partner was quick, and took immediate notice that I had caught on. "Keep your eyes in your head, American." She whispered. "Also, take your hand out of your bag. He will not be a threat."

The bag she referenced was the only thing that I had salvaged from the truck. Olivia had been quick to point out that my sword would be hard to hide without the bag that I had left to burn in the Andorra Inn. The new bag was slightly smaller but it had belonged to Robert, and had been filled with all of his things. It was just big enough for the scabbard and the pistol.

We turned down an alley close behind our quarry, and I was unsure whether or not he knew that we were behind him. If he had an ounce of the attention to detail that I had, then he should have noticed us by now.

He turned another corner and Olivia started to trot, taking the corner almost immediately after him and a step or two ahead of me.

Against Olivia's command, my hand was more than on my pistol as I drew it from the bag and rounded the corner.

The sight that greeted me was exactly as I had predicted. Our quarry had turned the corner in the alley and waited for our headstrong lady. As Olivia had rounded the corner, he had grabbed her and shoved her against the nearest wall. He held a short knife to Olivia's chest.

I recognized all this in the same instant that I rounded the corner. In a flash of movement, my pistol was pressed against his temple.

Without moving his head, Olivia's assailant looked at me through the corner of his eye. "You were right, Olivia. The American is fast."

I was confused and any soldier will tell you that confused is the worst place to be when you're about to do battle. My confusion led to hesitation and I did not pull the trigger.

"Put it away, Dr. Doran." Olivia said. "I knew that you would be incapable of listening to me if I told you not to draw your weapon." The attacker pulled his knife away from Olivia's breast and in a swift movement it was vanished from my sight.

Leaning away from the wall, Olivia waved her hand to indicate the man with the knife. "This is my contact in Lyon." He thrust out with his hand. "His name is Leo."

I slowly lowered my gun and put it back into its holster in my bag.

"And Leo is our...?" I pressed.

Olivia rolled her eyes. "He is our place to stay for the evening. Unless you'd rather sleep in the streets?"

"I've never seen the streets pull a knife." I mumbled and Olivia ignored it. Slightly louder, I said, "Then let's stop standing around trading baseball cards and get to this safe house." I looked away from Olivia and to Leo. "Where is this wonderful house of sleep?"

Olivia eyed me, and not for the first time I couldn't tell what she was thinking. I assumed that she was trying to read what thoughts I had toward this man or the method they had for finding each other. That was part of it. The other part, I was embarrassed to admit even to myself, was that I was wondering to what depth their relationship had gone before I was in the picture.

I had to remind myself that I knew nothing of Olivia and, aside from light flirting in the truck ride, I had no reason to assume that she had any interest in the 'American.' On top of that, I doubted that I was even interested in her. While she was a gorgeous woman, she was the first woman I had sustained any lengthy contact with since before my time with the Night Watchers. I was undercover with them for barely more than a year, and their ladies were into bloodletting and the sort. If I'd been traveling with a gun-toting granny, I am certain that I would have found her just as enticing as I was finding Olivia now.

On another side of an already too many sided coin, it was possible I was only being used as well. Feminine wiles were the oldest weapon in the arsenal for derailing a man from his mission. I had to stay ever vigilant, not jealous.

Thinking with a clear head, I still knew nothing about this Leo.

His French was heavily accented, more so than anyone that I had come across yet. When he spoke, it took me slightly longer to translate than it had for any of the other Frenchmen that I had run into.

"Yes," he answered. "It is this way. I think we could all use a drink."

"A little stronger than wine." Olivia added.

Leo flourished with a bow and indicated the rest of the length of this new bend in the alley.

We walked then and mostly kept quiet aside from Leo directing us down different roadways and alleys. We finally came upon a small residence tucked away behind several equally small shops.

We entered through a small front door and into a tiny kitchen. The entire home wasn't much bigger than the Dean's personal library, but I was sure that it was more than adequate for the purpose of hiding members of the Resistance.

I set my bag down on the small table in the corner of the kitchen and turned toward our host. "Are we the only ones here?"

"Tonight you are." He answered. Leo waved his hand to indicate the rest of the house. "Make yourselves at home. The owners are away in Paris, visiting relatives." He put his hands into his pockets. "There is one bedroom upstairs. I suggest that we give that to Olivia, while you and I take up places on the floor down here."

I nodded agreement. It wasn't only gentlemanly, it was also safer. Leo and I could watch the doors and Olivia would have fair warning if we were to get into any sort of entanglements.

Olivia caught this, too. "That is unacceptable. I do not need protectors. I will sleep down here and Leo can take the upstairs room."

He shook his head emphatically while I decided to remain uninvolved in the argument. I wanted to see how this played out.

"That was not a request." Leo replied coolly. "The upstairs will be safer." He smiled at her and shrugged. "We will need your fighting as our backup if we get into trouble."

Olivia stepped forward and slapped Leo across the face. Without saying another word she turned and stormed across the room and up the stairs.

Leo pulled his hands from his pockets and rubbed his face where Olivia had struck it. "That woman." He said quietly. "There is no winning with her."

"That is why I am grateful that she is on our side." I replied.

"Our side?" Leo asked. He'd obviously had a moment to talk to Olivia that I had missed.

"Well, her side. Your side. Not the Nazi's side." I folded my arms. "Whatever you might have heard about me, I am sure that you didn't hear I was a Nazi sympathizer."

Leo walked over to the little table and grabbed a chair. He turned it around and then sat down facing me. "I have heard very little of you, Dr. Doran. At the very same time, if I get caught by our enemies then I am sure that I know too much."

My arms still crossed, I encouraged him to continue.

"The word among our German friends is that an American is trying to get into Germany to steal a weapon. They say he's a Doctor, and they fear him. Even afraid, they still wish to catch him alive. It seems that they want him as badly as they want this weapon he seeks." Leo leaned forward then and put his hands on his knees. "The rumors within the Resistance tell a different story. They claim that this American is a wizard, sent from America to place a curse on the Reich." He leaned back again, his excitement replaced by a smug look. "You are the first American that I have seen who seems to be working his way toward Germany. So tell me, Dr. Doran: Are you man or wizard?"

A wizard?

I had never been called a wizard before. A practitioner, maybe. I've even been called an imp and, most frequently, a hack. Never have I been called a wizard, but for all intents and purposes, the argument could be made that I had more power than the average scholar. I'd read up on the wizards of old, though. The Necronomicon never shied away from the subject. Wizards of old held much more power than I ever had and they got it in much more sinister ways. My little bit of magic that I could control was based on knowledge that I had gained in my travels and from that dreaded book. The wizards of old had made deals with demons and beings from beyond reality itself. This gained them knowledge that the human mind was never meant to know. For this reason, they grew mad over time and after the madness, they would grow corrupt.

I was no wizard. A stage magician with a gun, yes, but a wizard? Definitely not.

I didn't say as much to Leo, instead telling him that I was only a man, but yes, my mission was not that of the French Resistance.

"Olivia and yourself are dedicated to the freedom of France. I respect that, but I'm not part of it. I have my own direction to travel." I explained. "If I can help the Resistance without jeopardizing my own mission, then I will. I have no love for the Nazis, but getting sidetracked will result in a much greater loss to the world than just France."

"Oh, hero?" He smiled up at me. "Is the world yours to save then?"

I only looked at him. He may have given us a house to stay in, and Olivia may have trusted him, but I didn't even know if I trusted Olivia yet. I owed his man nothing. "I'm going to bed." I turned and walked into the living room, scooping up my bag on the way.

I sat in a corner on the floor and rested my bag under my head. I then pulled my journal and my gun out, placing the gun next to me and began writing in my diary. When I had finished, I replaced it in the bag and attempted to drift to sleep.

I had been lying with my eyes wide open for about two hours when I first heard it. The sound was unmistakable. Someone was pounding heavily on doors and shouting in French. I couldn't hear the words, but they were angry.

Leo was already at the window with his own rifle in his hands. I hadn't known he had a rifle and silently wondered what other weapons had been hidden around the house.

"Stay quiet," Leo said without prompting. I had only grabbed my pistol and begun to rise.

Ignoring him, I said, "What is going on?"

He scowled but did not look at me as he answered. "They are sweeping houses. They're asking about trucks and an American." He looked at me then. "Word of your escape from Andorra has traveled almost as quickly as you."

Olivia was suddenly beside me with a tiny pistol in each hand. Standing beside her with only my magical .38 pistol, I suddenly felt the need to grab my scabbard.

"What do we do?" She asked. Leo looked at her, his face an unreadable mask.

"We use the traboules." It was a French word, but I had never heard it before.

"Traboules?" I asked, allowing my eyes to dart back and forth between Leo and Olivia.

"Secret passages," Olivia answered.

I nodded. "Good. I was just thinking to myself how much we could desperately use secret passages right now."

She frowned at me and I caught myself wondering if she'd learned the excessive use of that mannerism from Leo.

Leo pushed away from the window and moved between us and toward the kitchen. "They are coming this way and will be here after the next house. We must move quickly." He nodded the direction that he walked. "Traboules or fight?"

"Traboules," Olivia and I said in unison. I had no doubt that we could take however many were going to be knocking down our door, but to do so would be to give up a perfectly good safe house as well as make another person have to leave their home. Leo might have been grating on me, but I did not wish to boost him out of Lyon.

Or give him cause to join me and Olivia.

Leo didn't look back as we answered, instead continuing into the kitchen. I grabbed my bag and we followed him in silence. When I saw him struggling to move the heavy cast iron stove, I stepped to his aid and together we shifted it forward.

Behind it was a small hole in the floor, about the width of myself with only a few inches to spare. Beyond the hole was only blackness.

Leo quickly grabbed a military flashlight from a drawer and handed it to Olivia. Together, Leo and myself lowered her down by her wrists. The floor must not have been far. She was touching the ground while we still held her.

Leo waved me forward and I did not hesitate. With a quick leap I was through the hole and beside Olivia as she worked the flashlight.

As Leo came down, she aimed it at the hole and we saw a heavy iron bar that was attached to the base of the stove. Leo and I grabbed it and pulled the oven back into place.

With the oven now covering our entrance, I assumed us safe, and turned to walk down the tunnel. I took two steps when Leo grabbed my arm and stopped me.

"Don't move." He said.

He then yanked the flashlight from Olivia's hand and aimed it at my feet. I stood only one step from a deadly hole directly in the middle of the floor. It wasn't a hole from some sort of wear or tear on the foundation. This was a hole actually built into the floor of the tunnel. It had an edge that was beveled, but there were no stairs. It was only a straight drop.

I eyed Leo curiously, and his only response was "Protection, in case they follow us."

"This foundation is much older than the Nazi party." I said. "Who would you have had to run from before this?"

"It is not my home, wizard." He replied. His face said that he wasn't telling me everything. "France has a long history of uprisings. Perhaps you are not the first wizard to grace these halls with your presence."

I had no explanation for it then, but I found myself suddenly gripping my pistol tighter.

Olivia grabbed the flashlight back and, without hesitation, stepped around the hole to continue down the tunnel. Keeping my tight grip on my .38, I followed her and allowed Leo to take up the rear.

The tunnel seemed to continue forever in the endless blackness, but we only went another ten or fifteen feet before Olivia came to a stop and held a finger to her lips. "Listen!"

We did as she bade and we could hear the pounding on the front door of the house. Shouts began in French, quiet and angry, and quickly rose to a much louder volume.

I heard one of them shout that they had seen movement and that it was our last chance to open the door. It hadn't been a full count to three when the front door must have been kicked in, because I heard a loud crash and then we could hear them stomping around the house.

Leo looked away from the tunnel ceiling that we had all been staring intensely at and toward us. "They will not find the tunnel, we are safe if we stay in here for the rest of the night."

The flashlight, still in Olivia's hand, suddenly cast to the floor. Seeing nothing of a disgusting nature, Olivia sighed and plopped her bottom down on the cleanest looking corner.

"Find a seat and relax, American. The evening has just begun."

I took the flashlight from her and looked for another clean spot on the floor. My eyes saw that there was another beveled hole in the floor and I took the moment to look down into it. Even with the light in my hands, I couldn't see the bottom, but I could hear something, similar to a shuffle, shambling in the darkness and echoing up the hole. It was faint, but definitely there.

"Where do they lead?" I asked Leo, hoping for either a reveal of more knowledge or for a possible escape other than the oven entryway.

"I do not know." He sat down beside Olivia without looking to see what might be beneath him first. "This is not the only house that I have found them in. There are rumors that most of Paris is tunnels. I have no doubt that Lyon is the same way." I turned off the light then and sat down across from them and listened as he continued. "In Paris, they speak of the tunnels being of the dead.

I would not compare Lyon's tunnels in the same manner. I have heard of … things down here. Rumors of old witches and wizards that had created black sorceries in these caverns. There are many different tales about what lives down those holes."

With nothing better to do, I pressed him. "Such as?"

"The one that the children like to tell is that the holes are where the old wizards would spirit away the bad boys and girls and save them for dinner. The noises that you can hear are those stolen children, old and withered, praying for release from life." I heard Leo move, only slightly, and then he continued. "Another story talks of monsters, made from the parts of animals and man. They were kept down there so that the wizards and witches could conduct their dark experiments upon them. This story is the one that you hear in the taverns and brothels. The whores tell that the wizards and witches died of incredibly old age, but their monsters survived. The spells that were done to them gave them unending life and torment."

I could hear in his voice that he didn't believe either story. My own travels and experiences left me open to the possibility that either story could be true. It was easy to hear in Leo's voice that he thought them just legends for encouraging children to stay well behaved.

His voice also hinted that he did fear what was down those holes, so I asked him.

"What do you think is down there?"

Leo laughed. "What, wizard? You don't believe that monsters live under the streets of Lyon?"

I was certain that monsters did, in fact, live under the streets, and not only in Lyon. I didn't say as much. Instead I said, "It isn't what I believe: it's what the man who calls these streets home believes."

"Well said," was Leo's reply. The mirth had left his voice as he continued. "I am not very superstitious, but I have found that the only story that scares me is the one of the tombs." He became quiet for a moment and from overhead we could hear the Nazi soldiers tearing apart the furniture. "I believe that the tunnels were used by the wizards, but that through their dark practices they had found the path to immortality. The wizards fought among each other using their magic. During the last of their battles, many retreated into those holes but they couldn't get back out."

Olivia made a noise, and I imagined that she shivered then.

"There was a problem with their magic," Leo went on. "They had learned how to trap their souls in the realm of the living, but they hadn't figured out how to stop the slow decay of their bodies."

"You think those holes lead to the trapped and rotting bodies of the ancient wizards?" I asked him.

"I've heard more fanciful tales." He replied, but I could hear in his voice that whatever was at the bottom of those holes was something that terrified him.

Olivia spoke up then. "Yes, boys, please keep telling your scary stories while the Nazis hunt us and I try to sleep. This night was just beginning to become too light on my nerves..."

I laughed and Leo joined in. It was a nervous laughter brought on by our situation and I was sure that Olivia, for all of her brusque nature, had a smile across her face as well.

A crash and the sound of falling debris stopped our laughter instantly. The sound rang in my ears and I felt as if I had just been in the center of an explosion. I turned the flashlight in the direction of the entrance to the tunnel and saw dust and the looming forms of several men. The Nazis had found our tunnel escape.

Leo was beside me then and grabbed the light out of my hand. As he took it, he flipped the switch to keep it from giving our enemy a clear target. Together, the three of us took off down the tunnel and around a corner away from the Nazis.

Without the flashlight, I couldn't see where I was going, but I had seen two of the holes and they had both been in the center of the tunnel. I kept tight to the walls and continued to run forward, directly behind both Olivia and Leo.

Bullets suddenly came racing down the tunnel and smacking into the walls beside me. Spinning I shot three times over my shoulder. Their firing stopped but only for a second. I shot once more and then also stopped. They began firing again then, coming incredibly close to my head with their aim. The stone began to chip away and shower into my face as the walls became riddled with bullets. More out of reflex than anything, I dove forward.

That was my undoing. As I dove, I couldn't see where I was placing my feet and the shot so close to my head had left my sense of direction completely useless. It was one step and then a second and I couldn't feel anything under my foot on the third.

I fell, my bag and shoulder hitting the edge of the hole hard, and then I went down the hole.

With a sharp yelp, I began my descent. I placed my boots on the edge walls and thrust out my arms, hoping to slow down my fall. I knew that if I couldn't see the bottom than it was far enough at least to break my legs in the free fall. I said a quick prayer, begging whoever was listening to allow me to slow down enough not to land and become a puddle.

My boots suddenly couldn't touch the walls anymore, and in that same instant my arms were free of it as well. I fell for another ten feet or so before my legs slammed into a solid floor. The force went through my knees and hips, and no amount of bending my knees could absorb enough shock to stop me from feeling it all the way up my spine.

My bottom hit the ground in almost the same instant as my feet hit, and I was certain that I had broken my tail bone.

I laid on the cold ground for what seemed like forever before I decided to test out my legs and back. I hurt everywhere but, to my relief, nothing was broken and I could stand with only minimal discomfort.

Judging by the constant ache in my behind, sitting was going to be a horrible experience for the foreseeable future.

My bag had landed nearby and after feeling around in the dark I managed to scoop it up. Bending carefully over I also ran my hands over the floor in an attempt to locate my gun.

That was when I heard the howl.

I couldn't tell where it was or how close. The cavernous nature of the room that I had landed in made the echo reverberate and I couldn't tell if the creature who had howled was ten or a hundred feet away. I gave up on my search for the pistol and dug my hand into the bag, withdrawing the scabbard that held my magical sword. In a clumsy movement, I pulled the sword free and held the scabbard out in a defensive stance. The thing that howled made no further noise and the echo finally began to die down.

Once my ears had stopped ringing with that monstrous voice, a new noise filled them.

It was dry and sounded as though it was somewhere between a choke and a cough, but I had no trouble understanding it.

"Finally," said the voice. "You've … come…"

I shivered then; the voice scared me. Without a sound to indicate movement I was suddenly hit in the chest and thrown backward.

My sore tail bone hit the ground hard and I dropped the sword and scabbard. Before I could recover from the attack, the thing that had spoken was upon me. It wrapped bony appendages around my throat and began to choke the life from me. Groping, I found the handle of the sword and swung it gracelessly at my attacker. One of the appendages pressing down on my throat was struck by the blade and suddenly went limp. I felt it begin to liquefy and a thought floated into my mind then. Whatever this was, it had been touched by the void. My sword only did that nasty liquefy trick when it touched something of the void.

That was the last thought to go through my mind. Instead of reeling when I removed the thing's arm, it instead thrashed out with the other appendage. It smacked me directly in the forehead and everything went dark.

"Andrew!"

I woke to my name being called. I could hear it everywhere and I knew that I must still be in the hole.

To my surprise, I answered the call, but without moving my mouth. As a matter of fact, the voice was nowhere near me.

"Yes," my voice echoed. "I am down here. Do you have any rope?"

I heard Leo answer, "Yes!"

I was laying down, and I still couldn't see anything in the blackness. I was confused and worried that I had experienced a blow to my head. I didn't remember answering, but it had most definitely been my own voice.

I placed my right arm under me and sat up. My body ached in all sorts of new places, but not in my tail bone. That formerly sore place on my person had stopped hurting, making it easier to sit up than I had expected.

As I sat up, I looked around and was surprised to realize that I could actually see something.

Light was flashing down through the hole. I couldn't see much other than the inside of the hole being lit up, but I could see the light moving around within it.

Whoever was up above, and I assumed that it was Leo and Olivia by the voices, was trying to see whatever was down the hole. Then the light hit upon something that I couldn't completely understand. It was another person, and my immediate assumption was that it was the monster, but whoever or whatever it was had two arms ... and my pistol, which I recognized as the light from above glinted off the runes etched into its surface.

Working from the assumption that I had been capable of speaking only moments before, I tried to do so again. My intent was to let them know that I was not the only one down there.

"Gak ... glak..." My throat was incredibly dry and it felt as if I was choking as I tried to speak. When the monster had strangled me it must have caused more bruising than I had thought.

I saw the length of a rope as it came down through the hole; a loop had been tied into its end. The man with my gun grabbed the rope and set his foot into the loop. He held on with only one hand as it began to rise. The beam of light came down onto him more directly as he began to lift from the floor and I saw something that only added to my confusion: the man on the rope looked like me!

I placed both hands under me then and attempted to stand, except that wasn't what happened. As I placed both arms beneath me, I fell to my left without any support on that side. I hit my head hard onto the floor and let out a moan that sounded just as dry and raspy as my attempted speech had been. Groping blindly, I brought my right hand up and grasped at my left arm.

It had been cut off beneath the elbow.

I finally understood, as well as anyone could, what was going on.

One of those damned wizards or mutants or whatever they were had hijacked my body and meant to leave me down here to rot in his place.

You did not need to know the secrets of not aging if you knew the secret of hopping bodies.

It was a difficult spell to create, but I was lucky to have been the victim. The soul was shaped very specifically for everybody.

Squares could not fit in round holes without being forced. Thieves of bodies had to force their way in and they would have to deal with the shape being all wrong for them. For the victims it was simple, with only a little of know-how, to reverse the effects and bounce back into the proper body. All I needed to do was touch the being. Physical contact was key.

I raised my/his head up toward the light and my body was no longer visible. I ran the dried out tongue of the mouth I had been forced to use around inside of it and prayed that it had enough moisture for what I needed. Once I thought that the job had been accomplished, I shouted as loudly as I could.

"Stop…!" It was raspy, but the word came out. "Stop! Please! That is not your friend…" I broke off then in a coughing fit and tripped over something as I stood.

I felt around on the floor where I had tripped and something bit into the flesh of my only arm and I let out a small gasp of pain.

Aside from the cut nothing special happened though, and I reached down and felt for what had caused me the pain.

The hilt and the runes gave it away; I had found my sword, but it had not dissolved my flesh when it had cut me. The sword, for as much as a sword could, recognized me. I didn't know how, but this information might become useful in the future.

Finally bringing my new body more fully under my control, I did my best to sprint to the hole and looked up.

My doppelgänger, or hijacker, or whatever you would like to call it, was well beyond my reach, but I called out again.

"Olivia!" I took a deep breath. Yelling was very difficult and I was already feeling the toll on my withered and aged lungs. "Olivia! That is not the Andrew Doran that you are pulling … up…" I coughed uncontrollably then. "Please, drop him! Drop him now!"

My voice echoed from above me. "The demons are trying to trick you, Olivia! Quick! Pull me up before they try to grab me again." "Ask him!" I wheezed. My breath was getting harder to catch. "Ask him … from where … he hails!"

My last words were barely more than a whisper and I knew that my allies couldn't hear it. I collapsed from the staring of speaking so much and understood that using the power to switch souls must have drained the monster. He could have killed me when he had done the deed and then he'd have been in the clear to escape, but he knew that he'd need the strength just to make it up the hole and out of this damned crypt.

Out of the hole. If I could not get them to drop the body back down, I would be left with getting out of the hole myself. This wouldn't be easy if it was even possible. If it was simple the wizard would have crawled from the hole many centuries ago. I had to hope that I was somehow more clever than the century old wizard and that maybe I could come up with something that he did not.

I thought, then, upon the Dean Brandon Smythe's pet shoggoth and how it had moved me from the desert and to the halls of Miskatonic University. It was a wishful thought. I could not conduct a similar feat without losing complete control of my mind. I would enter the void as Dr. Andrew Doran, at least in mind, and would leave a monster befit his shell.

I rested there, beneath the hole on my knees and looking upward at the quickly rising form of my own body when I noticed something cold and hard in my grip.

In the grip of my left hand…

I looked down at where my left hand should have still been and stared at it intently. I rolled my wrist, and while nothing visible happened, I could feel my wrist roll. I had heard of phantom pains and feeling limbs when they were long missing, but this was different. I could feel something in my left hand. I slid the thumb of my left hand up and down what was in it and wiggled my index finger. My examination yielded interesting results. I was holding my rune covered .38 pistol.

Suddenly, I had a plan. The soul is a fickle thing. Laws of science don't apply to souls. Laws of the void don't even apply to souls, which is probably why shoggoths crave them so much.

Swapping the bodies after I had so recently cut off the wizard's arm with the magic sword had left me in control of a piece of my original body. My soul still had a left arm.

Maybe I wouldn't need magic at all. Maybe I could just … shoot something.

I liked this idea and it gave me a renewed energy.

The devil wizard's arm was cut off directly below the elbow, so I could only assume that any control I might have over my body's arm would be limited to only the wrist and my hand. It would have to be enough.

Using the rotted eyes in the soft skull of the dead wizard, I looked up the hole another time and this time I paid close attention to where the limbs of the body were situated.

Regretting it as I did it, I then moved my left wrist only barely, twisting the gun up and to the right.

Then I squeezed the trigger. The boom of the pistol filled my ears and the hole. As the ringing in my head subsided, I heard a howl of pain that was entirely inhuman coming from the shaft.

I looked back up the hole and was greeted with an excellent sight.

I was falling.

The wizard didn't have as far to fall as I had the first time, but he was still in my sore body. I let him hit the ground, hoping he hadn't broken any of the merchandise.

Before he could get up, I punched him hard in the base of the back, hoping that my tail bone was hurting him as much as it had been hurting me. His right wrist was bleeding, so I kicked it, flinching as I did. Getting back into my body looked like it was going to be a painful affair, and I wasn't making it any better.

I didn't know how I knew, but somewhere deep in the head of this long dead wizard's ragged corpse was a piece of a thought that he had left behind. I couldn't just touch his flesh with my flesh and hope the souls would trade again. It had to be something different.

Using the wizard's hand, I ripped open my own shirt. Then, taking my dead stump, I thrust the cleaved end against my own chest. To all watching, it would look only as though I were poking him in the chest with a rotten piece of arm, but he and I both knew it for what it was.

I had the soul of my hand deep into my own chest and once I had found what I was looking for, I tore it out of my body.

In the next moment a surge of confusion came over me. My perspective changed and instead of looking down on my own face, I was looking up on the face of a withered and ragged corpse. The eyes were nothing more than pinpricks of light that resided deep within the skull. Of the skull, a large portion of it was missing, exposing the rotten brain. How a soul could be housed in such a beast, I did not know.

The next sensation that washed away all the confusion from the soul shift was an intense pain that came across my entire body. Whatever the wizard did to keep his body alive and intact also kept it from pains. Returning to my body was a lesson in life itself. Life was pain, and rarely more so than when you've been beaten, shot, and dropped down a long shaft in a French cave.

Twice.

Something in the back of my mind shouted above the pain, only barely, and I opened my eyes in time to see the dark wizard making another lunge at me. I swung my recently rehoused arm back around and placed the pistol directly in his line of sight.

I'm unsure what kind of damage the wizard had prepared his body for. Could he and his soul remain in that body when it was nothing but ash and long forgotten particles? I had no idea, but I was certain of one very profound thing in that moment: he'd have to spend eternity doing whatever it was he did down there without his head.

Climbing carefully to my feet and cradling my shot arm, I took the sword from the dead wizard's body and replaced it in the scabbard and then into the bag. Then I walked back to the hole where someone was shouting down to me.

"I'm fine, just send the rope back down." I shouted back up. The flashlight beam came down on my face, and I was blinded for just a moment before the rope came down to my feet.

Sliding my foot through the loop and wrapping my unshot hand around the rope, I allowed my allies to pull me back up and through the hole.

Smoke and moans of pain were what greeted me back in the tunnel.

As Leo pulled me up, I noticed that Olivia wasn't around. I looked at Leo with exhausted eyes and said, "Where is she?"

The Frenchman only pointed. I followed his arm down the tunnel and saw that Olivia stood at the bend that we had gone around once the Nazis had followed us. She wasn't shooting, but had her gun up. The firefight must have raged on while I was in the other body, but I had been completely oblivious to it. Now, I could only assume that the tunnel and Olivia's own gun kept the Nazi soldiers from advancing.

I took a moment in Leo's lighting to check and reload my pistol. I then leaned on Leo and stood very carefully. The pains that arched up my legs were impossible to describe. I was surprised to be standing. When Leo saw my careful steps he gave me a look of concern mixed with disbelief.

I shrugged and gave him half of a smile. Both caused another shot of pain to course through my body. I was hurt, but we weren't out of the fire yet.

"What happened down there?" The Frenchman asked me.

"I'll explain later," I supplied. "Right now, we need to get out of here." I pointed in the direction we had been headed. "What's that way?"

Leo shrugged. "I have never had the chance to find out."

I nodded. "You will today." I looked toward where Olivia stood, reloading her gun. "We need them to follow us. Maybe they'll take a trip down one of those hell holes I found." I then moved to Olivia's side.

I touched her shoulder while she peeked down the way we had come from. She leapt at my touch and spun around. After a loud curse in French, she poked me in the chest.

"Where have you been?"

I jabbed her back. "You know right where I was, and you should just be grateful I'm back and not some damned monster in my place."

Olivia looked at me oddly then, a hint of understanding somewhere behind her eyes. I doubt she had any idea of what had just transpired, but she fully understood that it probably came from my world of dark monsters and not her world of Nazi spies.

I changed the subject. "How many?"

She shook her head. "Too many." Olivia leaned around the corner again and then brought her attention back to me. "They have stopped shooting for now, but only because they can't see me."

"Go with Leo. We need them to chase us. I think I can handle that."

She eyed me. "*Chase* us?"

"Yes. We want as many of them in the tunnels as possible. The more of them in the tunnel the less of them on the streets when we finally get out of here."

"Where do the tunnels lead?" Olivia asked me.

"Out, I hope."

"And what are you going to do that won't get you killed?"

I gave her the same half smile that I had given Leo only moments ago. "I'll improvise. You know: be American."

She rolled her eyes at me and left me alone at the bend so that she could join Leo.

I whispered to them then, hopefully not loud enough for the Nazis to hear. "Get ready to run." As an afterthought, I added, "Watch your step."

I could hear the soldiers ahead of me and knew they could hear me if I wanted them to.

Now, I wanted them to.

"I surrender!" I shouted in English. "Don't shoot, I'm coming out." I hoped that they had at least one person there who could understand it, otherwise this was going to be a horrible plan.

I set my bag down on the ground, just out of their sight around the corner I hid behind. Then I came around with my pistol raised and out, butt toward the Nazis, as if it I were handing it to them.

I walked toward them, slowly and limping of course, which I hoped added to the illusion of my having surrendered.

I could hear many soldiers but only saw one. I was relying on my being an American to confuse them and stop them from firing. It was my hope that they had been asked to detain any suspicious Americans instead of shoot them.

It looked as though my hopes had been justified, and once again I caught myself wondering how much harder my mission to Berlin was going to get. How did the Germans know of my mission? How many of them were prepared for my arrival?

The one soldier came at me slowly, his rifle at the ready. His form was one large silhouette, light from his companions streamed down the tunnel from behind him.

When he came within spitting distance I reached further out with the pistol, wiggling it a bit as encouragement for him to take it.

He nodded. He removed his steadying arm from the rifle's length and reached out for the pistol.

I moved then. I batted his rifle aside and stepped forward,

punching the Nazi in the face with the butt of the .38. His nose exploded in a shower of blood.

He lost consciousness immediately, but I didn't let that stop me from grabbing him and spinning him around to use as a shield.

His companions didn't hesitate to test out my makeshift shield as they filled the tunnel with gunfire. I felt the bullets as they punched into my makeshift shield and allowed the Nazi's body to take the brunt of the attack.

Bringing my pistol up on the now-dead soldier's right shoulder, I used their gun fire to locate the enemy and then placed several well-placed shots and continued to back away from them, careful to watch for the holes in the tunnel floor.

When I rounded the corner again, I carefully laid their companion down on the floor at an angle where he would be easily seen and almost directly in front of one of those treacherous hell holes.

I scooped up my bag then and took off in the wake of Leo and Olivia, being sure to keep as close to the walls and away from the pits as possible.

Surprisingly, I caught up with them very quickly. They were only shuffling along, seemingly giving me a chance to catch up.

We ran together for another moment or so before Leo found a ladder. At that same moment we also heard the first of what I hoped to be many gratifying screams.

Someone had just discovered a hole and, hopefully, a certain headless friend of mine.

We climbed the metal ladder quickly and came out in an alley between two of the houses only a short distance from the house we had been staying in.

"What do we do now, American?" Olivia asked me. There was no accusation in her voice. She was obviously grateful for the escape, but we couldn't stay in this alley for long.

"We need to get out of Lyon tonight." I said this and looked directly at Leo. Our contact wouldn't be much of a contact if he didn't have a plan for leaving in a hurry.

Leo nodded. "Start moving east." He pointed. "I know a man who can get us out, but I must find him. Continue east until I find you." He looked at Olivia then. "Do not worry. I will find you."

I was suddenly concerned, again, that Leo might be attempting to join our duo.

He took off down the alley and away from us. Olivia and I did not hesitate and together we began running east, sticking to the alleys.

We had gone about a mile when I collapsed against an alley wall. Hopefully the Nazis were going to be held up and too nervous about falling to follow us.

Olivia squatted next to me then and smiled. "I am happy to see you alive. First the hole and then your crazy plan against the soldiers. There is much to be said about your American ways."

I shook my head. "No, the American way is much milder than the Doran way, trust me."

What I saw in her eyes then made me wonder what exactly I was getting into in joining these new allies.

Olivia's eyes didn't show gratitude or romantic concern at my being alive any more than a craftsman would have showed gratitude that the hammer he thought long lost was surprisingly easy to find.

I saw my value in her eyes then. I was a means to an end for Olivia. For the first time since I had met her, I had no doubts as to where I stood with the French woman.

And now Leo was brought into this. I was becoming a tool of the French Resistance and I wasn't certain if this was a good thing or not.

Chapter 5: Geneva-Reanimated

I couldn't escape the feeling that I was no longer in charge of this cadre I had created. Reluctantly, I had allowed for the beautiful Olivia Fayette to tag along. It had been a decision born of logic more than sexual desire, although the desire was definitely there. Olivia had the ability to get me out of the nation of Andorra and more than halfway through Nazi controlled France with far less trouble than I would have faced on my own. For all her aid, I had to keep reminding myself that as a member of the French Resistance, she had her own agenda.

I wasn't too concerned about one gorgeous member of the Resistance. I knew that given the worst, I could handle whatever she threw at me, but, as Leo pulled up in a closed top French automobile, I was suddenly concerned that I was gathering quite the collection of Resistance members.

The car Leo had managed to acquire was beige with a rounded hood and rounded headlights. I didn't know cars, but I knew that this one would have been expensive.

Hardly a vehicle for traveling unnoticed.

The car had a backseat and a sloped rear window, but it had no doors for the backseat. Passengers would have to tilt the front seats forward and then climb into the back.

Hardly a vehicle that would be easy to exit if we're overrun.

I was beginning to question my faith in the Frenchman when he said the words that made me wonder why I had ever trusted him to begin with.

"We must hurry, they are right behind me."

I opened his door and stood aside with him looking at me with confusion. "Get out." I said. "I'm driving."

Leo looked at me for a moment longer before saying "Of course,

Dr. Doran," and then stepping out of the car. Tilting the seat forward Leo climbed into the back.

I had made the decision about five minutes before Leo had found Olivia and I stepping out of an alley about two miles from where he'd left us. I was in control of this group and, if Leo was going to join us, he needed to learn who was in control and soon. My demand of the driver's seat had earned me an evaluating look from Olivia, but I didn't acknowledge it. I wish that I could say that I didn't acknowledge her for the same reason I'd pulled Leo from the car, but I'd be lying. I'd ignored her look in hopes of impressing her with my cool command of authority.

Damn, she was too beautiful. It was going to get one of us killed.

I tossed my bag into the backseat with Leo and slid into the driver's seat. Once Olivia was in and the door was shut, I took off for the Eastern edge of Lyon.

We hadn't driven a block on the crowded city streets when Olivia called out.

"Up ahead!" Looking at where she indicated, there was a truck blocking the road with about ten soldiers standing outside of it, their rifles at the ready.

I had seen them as well, but her shout had definitely galvanized me into action. As the soldiers saw us and raised their rifles to their shoulders, I pulled the wheel to the left without slowing down.

Our car slid broadside to them and I gunned it, driving down a road perpendicular to our previous direction. The car rocked back and forth, and I could tell by Olivia's firing of her gun that we had someone following us. I didn't glance at the mirrors to confirm this. The alley was tight and I was crashing through bins and barely avoiding the few people taking refuge from the busy streets.

I touched the brakes for the first time as I saw the end of the alley approaching. Coming back out into the night, I turned the wheel to the right and continued toward the city's edge.

Our night had been a full one and as I drove east, I could see the first bits of orange streaking across the sky. The sun was coming up and it wouldn't be long before it was in my eyes. Hopefully it would be as much a hindrance to our pursuers as it was looking like it would be to me.

After taking the corner, I spared a glance into the mirror and saw that we were being chased by a singular military jeep. On board were only two passengers and a driver.

I'd only glanced in the mirror because the road was still crowded for early in the morning, but there was something about our pursuers that didn't sit easily in my mind.

Other than the whole shooting at us thing, that is.

I found our way out of the chase, and hopefully out of the city after leaving the alley. I was driving uphill and east which allowed me to keep the sun out of my eyes, but I was also coming to an area of town that had a large number of bins along the road. I cut into them at the crest of the hill. As the hood bashed into bin after bin they spilled into the streets. I continued over the hill and the sun blinded me for just a moment. I was grateful that the road continued straight. If there had been a wall or a bend in the road my trip to Berlin might have been put on permanent hiatus.

I could hear the crash from however far ahead of the enemy we were. They must have hit two of the bins, at least, but Olivia kept firing. I took my eyes from the road long enough to see that they had been slowed by the maneuver I had used, but only barely.

The edge of town wasn't far. I could now see the buildings thinning out. Through the buildings, the edge of town was well marked by two more jeeps with many soldiers lined up in front of them.

"Leo!" I shouted. "Gun!" I spared a glance at Olivia's back as she hung half out of her passenger side window. "Olivia, ahead of us!"

Leo passed me his machine gun while Olivia returned to her seat. Looking forward she shouted, "Zut alors, Doran!" *Damn it, Doran*, in French.

Rolling down my window, I took the machine gun in a one-handed grip and thrust it outside. Without taking the time to aim, I depressed the trigger. The roar filled the cab of the car more than Olivia's little pistol did. It was so loud that I didn't even hear Olivia's shooting, although I could see that she was miming me with her own gun.

The Nazis ahead of us scattered, diving behind their jeeps and off the road. I didn't slow the car at all and rammed the two jeeps that were blocking the road. Olivia and I managed to bring our guns in only barely in time and avoided losing our arms. In the backseat Leo was releasing a long string of curses.

Only a few of the soldiers had the wherewithal to remember that they were supposed to be stopping us and continued to shoot as they dove out of the way. The shots were mostly wide with only a few hitting the doors and the trunk. A loud sound of metal sliding across metal hit my ears next and holler of victory from Leo confirmed that we'd also lost our tail.

Keeping my eyes on the road ahead of and behind us, I continued to watch for Nazis. Why they hadn't chased us out of Lyon was a guess that I didn't dare hazard and Olivia and Leo voiced no assumptions either.

We had been driving for what seemed like hours, but a quick glance at my watch told me it had only been thirty minutes, when Leo asked the inevitable question.

"Where are we going?"

I liked this. I liked that they had no idea where we were going. That had been a clever preparation on my part. When Leo left to get us a ride, I had thought back on meeting up with Olivia. I had told her my journey would take me into France, and I had told her that I was headed to Germany. The next thing that I knew she had us meeting with her contact in Lyon. Someone who was ready for us and had knowledge of my arrival before we had even entered Lyon. I wasn't alright with this. They were my allies, as far as I could tell, but I had no idea how long that would last. More importantly, Olivia's preparation for our arrival had put me in the uncomfortable position of being outnumbered. I was driving a car of the French Resistance with two of its members sitting beside me.

In not telling them my next step until this moment, I was certain that they wouldn't have been able to have anybody in waiting to help, join, or otherwise sidetrack my mission.

I didn't want to keep them in the dark entirely. They had been helpful so far, and I could be completely wrong in my assumption of their intentions, but I couldn't afford to take that chance. Not yet.

"We're going to Geneva."

Olivia gave me a look of doubt. "Switzerland?"

I nodded. "My reasons are two-fold," I explained. "First, Geneva is the most direct path between myself and where I believe the book is being held. Being in neutral territory will give us a chance to relax as well. We'll be able to breathe and get our bearings before continuing on."

Leo leaned forward, resting his arms on mine and Olivia's seats. "Book? This is all for a book? The Germans burn books you fool!"

Leo was angry and this was the first time he'd heard of any of the details of my mission.

I decided that the Germans were already spreading the rumors of my movements and that it would do me no damage to explain a little further to Leo.

"Have you ever heard of the Necronomicon?" I asked him.

The Frenchman shook his head.

I continued. "It is a book of unimaginable power. The Germans think that with it they can rule the world." This was the very simplified explanation. "It was stolen from an American University. It is my job to get the book and return it." I waited for the other shoe to drop. I had just told Leo that the Germans have an American book that could turn the tide of the war. I had also told him that I want to put it back into a library.

"How can a book change the war?" I could see the wheels turning in Leo's mind. He was already thinking of how he could use this book himself. Of how the Resistance could stop the Nazis cold.

On the surface of it, I couldn't argue with his thinking. A weapon that could put the Nazi menace back into its bottle would be invaluable, but Leo didn't understand exactly what kind of powers existed in that book. The dreaded Necronomicon, even in the "right" hands, was a force of the darkest evils. If used by heroes or villains it would only summon Hell on Earth. To do that only benefited the demons of the world. The only safe use of the book was to not use it at all.

Much to my surprise, Olivia jumped to my rescue. "Book, brick, or mud: The Nazis think it is a weapon. Taking it back from them would show them that they don't have the world in the palm of their hand."

I nodded and decided against elaborating. Olivia knew exactly what kind of power this book had and instead of encouraging Leo's train of thought, she'd downplayed the importance of the book. She'd done what my sheer honesty would have failed to do: she had fanned his skepticism and now I could see the hope in his eyes fading.

I was no fool. That hope would stay and hum incessantly in the back of his mind. He'd keep telling himself that it was only a book, but the moment that we were close enough to finally grab the Necronomicon Leo would sense its real power. That would be an interesting day indeed.

Leo broke into my train of thought. "And the other reason for our trip to Geneva?"

I sighed. "I'm not exactly sure that I know where the book is."

I could tell by Olivia's eyes that she was not going to be coming to my aid this time.

"I know that the Germans will need to take the book to a group called the Traum Kult and I am also certain that the Traum Kult headquarters is in Berlin. What I do not know is whether or not the attention that the book has drawn might have encouraged them to move it to a more private location."

Olivia asked, "How will going to Geneva give you the location of the book?"

I shook my head. "It might not, but it's our best bet. I have a friend who is in Geneva. He's a priest and his name is Father Blake Fredericks. I met him a few years ago." I had met him during very bloody circumstances that had threatened not only his life but the lives of most of the people along the coast of the Gulf of Mexico. "Before he was a follower of God, he was a follower of Cthulhu and a member of one of the largest and most devout groups of Cthulhu worshipers in the world." I kept it to myself that he almost succeeded in raising the dreaded tentacled one from his slumber in R'lyeh. "He has since become a force for good, but he keeps his ears to the ground. If the Traum Kult has the book, then it is very likely that he will have heard."

Olivia's look of uncertainty continued. "And if he does not know where this book is?"

I shrugged, "Then the plan remains the same. I go to Berlin and I get back the book." I wondered to myself if they noticed that I hadn't said "We go to Berlin." If they did, they made no mention of it.

"Father Blake will know something." I added. "Of this I am sure."

At that moment, the sound of gunfire filled our ears.

I ducked instinctively but saw the plumes of gravel as the road took the brunt of the firing. I looked over my shoulder and saw that we hadn't escaped our Nazi tail as well as I had hoped. Doing a quick count I saw two military jeeps and one large truck with a canvas backing. Most likely there would be troops in the back of the truck. Troops with guns.

Looking ahead, I saw that the road branched off to the right. No sooner had I seen it when both Olivia and Leo shouted and pointed at it. As we came up to it, I yanked the wheel and sent the car careening down this new side road.

The gunfire was relentless and continued as the Nazi vehicles followed us. We had managed to avoid the bullets that came at us by sheer luck at this point so I began to weave back and forth across the road, giving our pursuers a moving target. The combination of the car's light weight and the shifting gravel on the road turned this maneuver of mine into a tactic that could be as hazardous to us as driving in a straight line. It became very difficult to keep the car under control. To counter this, I stopped yanking the wheel strongly either way and instead moved into a slight drifting pattern left and right over the road.

As I brought the car under a more calm control, Olivia leaned out of the window, as she had in Lyon, and began firing. My weaving didn't scare off the most forward of the jeeps and it slid up next to us on Olivia's side. She continued to fire and I saw the driver take three shots directly to his abdomen.

Olivia's bullets didn't affect the driver at all.

I took my eyes from the road only a moment longer to take a closer look at the driver. He was pale and didn't take his eyes off the road at all. His mouth was wide open and moving in a very slow chewing motion, as if he was trying to remember how to speak. The most off-putting thing about him was the large stitches all over his visible flesh. His head seemed to be sewn directly to his chest, with no actual neck between the two pieces. I moved my eyes across the rest of the jeep's occupants and realized that they all suffered in varying degrees to the same conditions afflicting the driver.

They were all dead.

A few years back, I had heard of a man who had done some very sick experiments on the battlefield during The Great War.

This man, Herbert West, had been a medic and had been cited as having collected the recently dead soldiers that came in from the front lines. He believed that he could reanimate the dead bodies. It was his hope to beat death as if it were a disease. He had gone missing soon after an incident with a superior officer. The reports were vague, but from what I could gleam from them, Dr. West had succeeded in reanimating the corpse of his superior. The results had been horrific.

Over the years there had been a scattering of reports around the world of similar events. People long thought dead would be suddenly up and moving about before vanishing completely.

Looking at this jeep of dead Nazi soldiers determined to destroy us, I had a vague idea of where Dr. Herbert West might have vanished to.

As the jeep pulled closer to us, Olivia moved to pull herself back into the car, but her movement was too slow. The Nazi soldiers grabbed her then. I heard the shattering of glass and the sound of gunfire suddenly filled the car as Leo began shooting at the jeep from his window. It was to no use, Olivia was pulled from the car, and before we could react the jeep had slowed down and fallen behind its fellow Nazi vehicles.

As the jeep fell back, the gunfire slowed but did not stop completely. I didn't see why until it was too late. A jolt ran through the entire car and Leo let out a loud bark of curses. I looked behind us again and saw that the large truck was successfully ramming us from behind.

The truck hit us again and I almost lost control of the car. They had Olivia and they couldn't be killed through conventional means, I was on the verge of panic as the car started to shift in the gravel. I returned to pulling the wheel hard to the left and then the right, purposefully fishtailing the car in an attempt to stop the truck from ramming us again. It was a useless attempt. Whatever the monstrosity was that currently drove that truck, it was diligent in keeping with its target.

I heard another shattering of glass and a quick glance told me that Leo had knocked out the rear window. He didn't try to aim, instead taking his machine gun and sweeping it from side to side out of the window. The roar of the bullets filled the cab of the car again, and to help my ally I stopped swerving the car. The bullets, as I had dreaded, had no effect on the large truck or any of its occupants.

"Leo, I need you up front." I shouted over the roar of his gun. "I need you to take the wheel."

Leo didn't question my demand, instead clumsily moved himself over the center console and into the front seat. He dragged his machine gun with him, although I doubted he'd get a chance to use it.

"Pass me my bag." I said to him after he sat in Olivia's former seat. He did so, and I pulled my magical .38 pistol from it. Leaving the holster in the bag, I instead leaned back and slid the pistol into the waist band of my pants. Without looking to see if Leo was ready, I said to him, "Keep her steady," and then slid out of the window of the driver's side of the car.

As I slid out, I grabbed the smooth roof of the car and attempted to find purchase. It wasn't easy, but with my legs propelling me I was able to climb onto the roof of the car. Holding tightly to the roof, I looked up at my quarry.

The truck's cab had a driver and a passenger. As I had expected, both were of the recently revived. Upon noticing me, the passenger of the truck leaned out of his window, bringing his gun forward to take aim at me. He looked about to shoot when the driver waved him off. Then, with a smile that only the dead could produce, the driver accelerated the truck.

I had been hoping for this. I carefully shifted to standing position on the truck, no longer gripping the sides.

The truck propelled itself toward us and the moment before it hit the back of the car, I stepped forward and jumped.

The truck hit the car with another screech of metal that I know sent Leo's teeth chattering. I was airborne and a living cannonball aimed at the windshield of the truck.

I rolled as much as I could midair and placed my shoulder directly in line with the window. I hit it hard and felt it reverberate through every pain my already well-taxed body had sustained over the last 48 hours. The window didn't shatter. Instead a large spider web shaped crack spiraled out of where my shoulder had impacted.

Hitting the windshield had put me in a bit of a daze and as I came back to myself, I looked up just in time to see the dead passenger raising his gun to shoot me through the cracked windshield. I rolled and slid toward the driver's side of the hood then, allowing myself to fall off the side of the truck, but not before looking for something to grab. My hands found purchase on the mirror located on the driver's side of the truck. I used my momentum from falling from the truck to swing my waist and legs up and onto the platform beneath the driver's side door.

No sooner had I found my footing when the reanimated driver unlatched his door and swung it open. He'd done it with remarkable force and I only managed to stay with the vehicle because I still had a hand on the mirror. In an effort to shake me off, he tugged on the door and slammed it shut again.

I managed to get my feet up on the platform again, but I did not give the driver time to do his trick again. Instead, I released the mirror and leaned through the driver's open window. I only pressed my arms and chest through, just enough to grab the driver around the back of the head and pull him toward the window.

My attack did little to even move the monster. Since I couldn't drag him out the window, I instead began shifting my energy to slam his face against the steering column.

One, two, three hits later and not a sign of blood from the corpse's ragged face and the monster wasn't even phased by the hits. It was then that he kicked the door open again. His idea had been to shake me off, but I had a better one. I continued to hold his head in my arms and as the door swung open I used his force to pull him from the seat and with the door.

Hanging from his head on the outside of the door, his body hung from the inside and he thrashed and kicked, causing the door to swing wildly. His passenger must have grabbed the wheel then, because the truck didn't shift from course, still riding close to Leo's car.

As we swung on the door, I began punching, with all my strength, at the back of his neck.

I was finally rewarded when the body of the dead thing that had been a Nazi soldier fell from the truck but his head was still in my arms.

The door swung shut again, of which I was grateful. I placed my feet again on the door's platform and looked into the cab. The passenger had moved over to the driver's side and was pulling back to punch at me. Before he could throw his fist, I pitched his companion's head through the window and into his face.

While he was distracted, I used the driver's door as a ladder and climbed onto the truck's cab. Once again attempting to keep my footing, I crouched and looked to the back of the truck.

I was greeted with two specific details of note. The first was that the jeep that had taken Olivia had fallen to the back of the pack. She was unconscious or dead, but seeing as all the dead things around there had been shooting at me, I was going to place my hopes on unconscious.

The second thing that I noticed was the five dead soldiers climbing onto the back of the canvas truck top and toward me. It was then that I pulled my pistol from my waistband. I aimed at the nearest crawling dead thing and was about to shoot when the truck swerved and almost knocked me off. I slid toward the passenger side of the truck and only barely stopped myself from falling. I wasn't going anywhere on this truck with the new driver trying to remove me. I had to do something different.

Still crouched, I placed three bullets into the cab above the driver's side. After the third bullet entered the roof, the truck slid and I knew that I had killed the beast.

I jumped to my feet then and ran toward the back of the truck. I took large steps and avoided the canvas in places that didn't have the solid frame beneath. Using the frame as stepping stones, I ran past the crawling and sliding dead Nazis as they reached out for me and jumped off the back of the truck just as it left the road.

Once again flying through the air, I had hoped to fly through the air and land amidst the first jeep. Unfortunately, leaping from a speeding truck driven by a second dead monster isn't something that people get a lot of practice at. Fortunately, I hadn't missed the jeep by much.

As I vaulted over the jeep I managed to grab the strap of a machine gun that was around one of the dead men in the backseat. My legs hit the gravel, but I was saved by the dead thing staying seated in the truck. I wasn't sure how I was going to get my legs off the gravel road and into the jeep, but I thankfully didn't have to figure it out.

A grip that was stronger than almost anything I had felt before suddenly grabbed me by the back of the neck and swung me into the jeep. The jeep was filled with four of the undead things, with one driving and the other three riding as passengers. As I landed in the lap of the soldier who had inadvertently saved my life the three unoccupied soldiers began to hit me.

To my surprise, I still had my pistol with me and I swung it forward and began to empty it of the last three shells. I took the first two soldiers in the head, returning them to their inert state, but my third shot went wide and missed the final monster. I kicked him away from me and slid the magical .38 into my waistband again. The first monster that I had killed happened to be the one with the loose machine gun strap. I grabbed the gun off him and filled the monster I had kicked off me with bullets. I started at the abdomen, but remembered that the bullets hadn't done any damage to these things until they'd struck the head. Remembering that, I kept the trigger depressed and raked it up the body toward his head. The gun stopped firing suddenly. A quick glance told me that it was jammed. I spun it around then and, burning my hands on the barrel, swung it at the monster. I connected with his gun hand and sent his weapon flying away.

He grabbed my machine gun from my burnt hands and threw it on the floor boards. We both stood in the jeep, balanced carefully on the seats as the driver mindlessly drove on.

The monster leaned forward and swung at me. It was fast, but I had seen it coming and ducked it. I then came up and, cupping my fists together, knocked him once and then twice against the chin. A normal man would have been down for the count on the first of those hits, but the animated corpse standing before me didn't even flinch. Instead, he thrust out his own fist with remarkable speed and caught me on the chin, rattling my jaw. His second swing, which I didn't even see coming took me right under my left eye and dropped me back and onto my butt.

I kicked up then, taking him first in his groin with enough force to make a living man pray for death and then twice more in the stomach. I took the small second it took him to register that I had kicked him to stand back up. Once I was on my feet, I began punching him as hard as I could in the face. It would have been more productive to punch a brick wall. He took each hit and then grabbed my wrist in mid-swing. He lifted me up and off my feet by that arm and then brought his fist into my stomach repeatedly. I'd lost count of the punches when a jolt in the running of the jeep made him drop me.

I looked up and noticed that Leo had slammed the brakes of his car, causing the jeep to ram them. I tried to stand but fell back into the seat. Trying again, I barely managed to square off against the monster. He seemed to be smiling.

I shouted, hoping that Leo could hear me. "Do it again!"

He must have heard me or the timing had been just right, because the Frenchman slammed on his brakes again and the jeep rear-ended the car. I jumped forward and tackled my assailant. My mass and the sudden deceleration of the jeep sent him reeling backward. As I landed on top of him, I made certain to aim at his neck as best as I could, landing it directly on the frame of the windshield. His head rolled down off the hood of the jeep and I collapsed in the passenger seat as the chase started up again.

The mindless driver continued onward as he sat next to me, completely oblivious to my now being the only occupant to his vehicle. I reached behind my seat and grabbed the fallen machine gun and set to work unjamming it. Once I had believed I'd succeeded, I tested it on the driver and then slid into his position.

I was tired, shot, hurting everywhere, and hadn't slept in longer than I cared to admit. It was time to end this.

I slammed on the brakes. The jeep with Olivia in it was far enough behind me that it didn't crash into me. The dead driver pulled the jeep around and took off after Leo. I sped up once the car was past and got very close to the back of the other jeep.

The clever Frenchman caught on and slowed his car down. Once the jeep had caught up to him, and prepared to ram him, Leo depressed his brakes and allowed them to. I used that moment and gunned the engine, ramming their jeep with as much force as I could put behind the military vehicle. It was a risky move, because none of the rotting monsters would have been any more affected by the jarring accident than they had been by the gunshots. It also had the severe risk of harming or killing Olivia, but at this point we were out of options. We couldn't shoot at them without risking hitting our French damsel, and I couldn't get close enough to take the jeep as I had this one without getting shot. The surprise of an overturned truck can only fool the dead once.

As soon as the jeeps and the car had all come to a stop, I scooped up the machine gun and jumped from my vehicle. Much closer to the jeep now, I had no fears about shooting and emptied the entire machine gun into the dead things sitting with Olivia. Leo joined me in the midst of the mayhem and helped me drag Olivia's still unconscious form from the vehicle.

Together we allowed Olivia to get some air and come to on her own, even though we both knew that this reprieve from action might not last. When she finally came to, we explained what had happened. She looked unbelievingly at me as Leo explained what he had managed to see me do from the mirror of his car.

"I guess there is much more to you than guns and books, Andrew." She said as we all seated ourselves back into the car.

I smiled a very sore and tired smile at her then. "I can cook, too." Olivia returned my smile and Leo changed the subject.

"If you don't mind, Dr. Doran, I'll drive while you recuperate in the backseat."

I agreed without hesitation. I doubt I could have kept my eyes focused on anything let alone the road at that moment.

Getting into Switzerland ended up being a simpler task than anything that we had come across so far. Olivia and Leo's connections within the French Resistance got us across the border and into neutral territory without any trouble at all. Once across the border, we all began to breathe easier and weights that had been riding on all our shoulders simply melted away. For the first time since I had met her, I heard Olivia's laugh and it was as bright and energetic as the look in her eyes would have suggested.

The last of the drive to Geneva took only another thirty minutes and we got there just in time to see the citizens moving about their mornings.

We asked only two people where we could find Father Blake Fredericks and they both directed us across Geneva and to a small hut with crosses on the door. The untrained eye would have seen those crosses and thought that was the end of it. I knew better. My eyes caught the warding symbols of the Necronomicon etched in the wood near the roof. This was definitely the place the old preacher had come to repent for his sins.

Father Blake greeted me with a hug that sent aches through my aches, but I accepted it greedily.

Olivia and Leo were greeted in much the same manner, with the Father winking at me when he pulled away from Olivia. I leaned toward him and whispered.

"You're to be atoning for sins, not creating new ones," and I winked back.

He shrugged and laughed. "No one is perfect. Not even you, Andrew."

We all sat then and the Father fed us. Over dinner I explained what had brought us here and everything that had transpired since leaving Miskatonic. Some of what I had to say was new to my companions as well, and they listened with rapt attention. The Father, while American by birth, understood French, and we conversed in that language so as to not alienate my allies.

When I had finished, Father Blake crossed his arms. "I'm sorry, my friend, but I don't know if I can help you." My heart fell. I did not look forward to going into Berlin blind.

"But," he said. "I think I know who can." He grabbed a roll of bread from a basket at the center of his small table and started talking over mouthfuls of bread. "You were correct. I have heard of the book falling into German hands. I have also heard of many greedy beasts screaming their jealousy from the rooftops. Some of them have even threatened to join the Nazi menace in hopes of at least catching a glimpse of your cursed book. As for where it could be, your estimate sounds the most likely. The Traum Kult are owned by the Nazi party, and the book could only be used properly by them." He took a swig of his drink. "Rumors and guesses are all that I have to offer, but I know who can help you. There is a scientist in Bern, two hours east of here. His name is Karl Freeman." He grimaced as if the name caused him pain. "He is American like us. I knew him from … my old life. He still lives with his beliefs and won't be easy to persuade to help you, but I think you'll get a more specific answer out of him. He's odd, and you should be cautious of anything he says to you."

"Bern?" Olivia asked.

Father Blake nodded. "It is an old city, with many..." he looked at me then, "secrets. I suggest you all stay here for a day or two and see to your wounds. Maybe you could get a little rest before moving on."

I was eager to get to Berlin, but I had been running on no sleep for too long. I had also been dragged through hell and back in regard to what my body had gone through and was unsure if I would last another day.

No matter how eager I was, the rest would be more than welcomed.

Chapter 6: Cool Air in Berne

Two nights in the company of Father Blake was two years too short with the jovial father. I had forgotten how much his attitude had lightened when he no longer begged for the rise of Cthulhu. Father Blake loaned us his car, under the condition that we promise not to tell anyone where we picked it up.

Even in Switzerland, trust had become a rare commodity.

We drove for a little under two hours before we found ourselves deep in the city of Berne. It took us another hour of questioning the locals before we located an address for Karl Freeman. The locality of Berne was not very excited at the mention of Karl Freeman, and I was surprised by the relief this caused inside me. Father Blake had claimed that Karl Freeman was a member of the Cult of Cthulhu. Well, he was a member of at least one of them. The cults were many and widespread. Some didn't even know that they were followers of Cthulhu, and others were primitive by means of technological advancement but thousands of years in advance of us in spiritual worship.

My relief had found home in the fact that if the people of Berne were hesitant to talk about Karl Freeman, then he must be a scary man to know. That meant Father Blake had been right; Karl Freeman was the man who could tell me about the location of the Necronomicon.

Leo had decided that he'd had enough of old men and dropped us off at the address to go find a place for us to stay. Hopefully, he'd also find us a way into Germany, but I decided to worry about that later. Leo hadn't been speaking much since he'd learned about the existence of the book. I doubted that he thought of it as anything more than a tool to be bartered with, but he knew that the Germans valued it, and that gave it value to the French Resistance.

I still had my doubts concerning his motives, but there was nothing that I could do about it then.

He left us in front of a short apartment building. It looked ancient and from the outside, Olivia and I could tell that most of the apartments were empty. The building was made of large stones and the roof had no slant to it. If I had to muster up my courage to enter, it was only to get past the dilapidated exterior.

Pushing my fear of structural inadequacies aside, I marched toward the door. I didn't make it two steps before Olivia grabbed my arm.

"I don't like it." She said through eyes that projected deep fear.

"Don't like what?" I asked.

"This man, this building, this city." Olivia looked at me then, instead of the building. "You're the one with the magical toys, can't you feel the … evil?"

I reached out with my mind, but even I couldn't sense much of anything from this distance. I could feel what room Karl Freeman was in, but only barely. Whatever relationship he had with the Old Ones, his connection wasn't a strong one.

It surely wasn't anything that someone with as weak a connection as Olivia should be able to sense.

"I sense nothing." I eyed her. "You can wait outside, I should be safe."

Olivia shook her head. "No, if you're going in, I'll follow." The look on her face was of unease and pain. I was unsure if it was pain at first, but a second look told me that whatever she was feeling, it caused her actual pain.

I took the stairs two at a time once we entered the apartment complex. Olivia took them a little slower, but I'd already decided I wasn't letting anyone slow down my mission.

The energy I'd sensed was on the third, and top, floor of the building. We came up on the landing and I slowed my pace to approach the door. As I touched it, the door pushed open, slowly. It was unlatched and I found myself wondering if maybe Olivia had sensed something that I should have. I glanced back at her and was surprised by what I saw.

Olivia was drenched in sweat and had grown sickly pale. She looked as if she was about to collapse.

I grabbed her around the shoulders. "What's going on?"

She shook her head with effort. "I don't know." She straightened then. "I'll be fine. Do what you have to do. I'll ... guard the door."

I smiled at her then. "Just like the French."

She returned it only half-heartedly. "Don't make me shoot you, American."

I turned from her then and back to the door. I'd left my scabbard in the truck again, trying not to draw any attention to myself, but I wore my holster and the magical .38. I wouldn't feel safe unless I had both weapons, but I couldn't have the best of both worlds.

Putting my hand on the door, I gave it a shove with my left hand as my right hand fell to the pistol. As the door creaked open, I was greeted with a blast of cold air from inside the room. There were no lights on in the cold room, but I could hear the whirring of a small motor and could smell something chemical.

The blast of air that had greeted me at the door stayed with me inside the room. The entire apartment was at least 40 degrees cooler than the corridor outside. I assumed that the room was kept at that temperature by the mechanical sound I could hear.

I took two more steps into the dark room before I was halted by a sound that I could not make out. I drew my pistol and held it up, prepared for the worst.

"Is anyone home?" I tried my best to peer into the blackness, but it did me no good. I was just about to take another step into the room when I was startled by a dry voice calling out.

"Stop." It said, and I was unsure at first if it had even said that much. The voice sounded as if it was incredibly parched. A glass of water would go above and beyond in aiding the speaker, I was sure. "Stop." Louder and stronger this time. "Please. Do not come any further."

I did not want to give any knowledge away without getting any in return. Instead of asking if it was Karl Freeman, I only asked, "Who are you?"

"You know very well that I am Karl Freeman, Dr. Doran. I left the door unlatched so that you would be able to enter without me having to walk to the door. I expected no visitors today other than yourself." There was no discernible accent in Mr. Freeman's voice. Wherever he might call home, I had no doubt that he had originally come from a predominantly English speaking country, and most likely America.

I hesitated before asking, "You expected me?"

He made a noise that sounded more like choking, but which I assumed must have been a laugh or snort. "You know of my background, Doctor. Please don't play me for a fool." He was quiet for a moment, but I could sense that it wasn't my turn to talk yet. "While I might not be able to predict the weather, I have no trouble when it comes to men of considerable means paying me a visit."

The background that he was referring to was that of a worshiper of Cthulhu. To open your mind to Cthulhu's dreaming projections was as likely to threaten your sanity as rubbing a match against the grain was likely to cause flame. It was argued in philosophical circles that if you were able to come out of the experience with most of your faculties still under your control then you'd be capable of feats of the mind such as predictions or telekinesis. The other side of the argument was that no one who accepted the dreaded lord Cthulhu as their leader would ever again have enough sanity to be within control of their own faculties.

"As a matter of fact," Karl continued. "I expect a great many things..." He let his voice trail off, and I waited for him to continue. "Is she in the hall?" He spoke up.

I could only assume that he had sense the arrival of Olivia as well as myself. "Yes. She felt ill at ease and preferred to stay in the hall."

Karl Freeman let out that dry wheezing cough sound again and this time it was loud enough that I could hear some resemblance to a laugh. "Ill at ease, I am sure." He paused again. Whether he continued these pauses for effect or for breath I did not know. "Her kind will find that it is not welcome here."

No matter how I worked my mind around it, I knew that he did not mean the French when he had said "her kind." I was suddenly in deep dread of my companion, but didn't let it show. Instead, I asked, "Women? The French? What kinds are not welcome here?"

"French is she?" He asked. "I'm sure ... yes. That would make sense. No, Dr. Doran, by her kind I am referring to lies."

"Lies?" I pressed.

"Yes," Karl rasped from his hidden corner. "This room is the pinnacle of truth and only truth can find a home here. Lies are veils and in this room there are no veils. All is bared for the guests to see."

It was my turn to snort. "No lies? Why can't I step closer? Why can't I see you? You choose to skirt the truth but insist that no lies will be found here?" My anger was rising in my throat and I almost stepped forward then.

"You could, but I ask that you do not. Not out of some sort of misdirection, but more out of embarrassment on my behalf." He took a deep breath and it was loud enough to hear across whatever distance stood between us. "I currently suffer from a condition that does not always show me in the best of terms. It is slightly worsened today and I wish that you not see me like this."

"Your condition?" I asked.

He hesitated. "If you press me on this, I will describe my condition in great detail, but the walls," he paused again, "are listening, and this is not the time of true knowledge. Tonight, at one in the morning, return to me and I will tell you everything that you need to know."

This was only another thing to put off my getting to the book. I was tired of set-backs and waiting. "I only need to know where the book is."

I wasn't sure if it was Karl Freeman or whatever the machinery was, but I heard a hiss then. "No. You need to know many more truths than the location of the Necronomicon. Tonight you will come to me, and come alone. She will try to accompany you, and that cannot be allowed."

I sensed the end of the conversation had come, whether I wanted it or not, and I wasn't going to risk losing all my answers by forcing a diseased old cultist to tell me his secrets. I didn't say anything as a farewell, instead choosing to holster my gun and exit through the doorway. I latched it behind me.

Olivia stood at the far end of the hallway still with a pale look that told me the answer to my next question. "Are you alright?"

She brushed it off by quickly saying, "Yes. Did you speak with him?"

I nodded. "Yes." After the little bit that Karl had mentioned regarding Olivia, I wasn't sure if it was meant to sow distrust or enlighten me. Either way, I couldn't ignore my new concern. Up until this point, I'd been worried about her allegiance to the French Resistance getting in the way of any sort of trust we could have. Now I had to worry about if she was ... what? Something from the void? That was jumping to conclusions. Maybe Karl was only sensing my own distrust. I chose to avoid telling Olivia about any of the discussion between myself and Karl, not even about meeting him later that night.

"Let's go see if Leo found us a place to stay." I said, changing the subject.

To our luck, Leo was waiting for us outside the apartment building in Father Blake's car. Leo had been busy in the short time since he'd left us. In the back of the car were ammo boxes and rations, both of which Olivia and I were more than grateful for. He also mentioned that he had managed to secure us transport into Germany on the next day. This meant to me that whatever business I had with Karl Freeman couldn't be put off any longer than it already had.

On top of those two very incredible feats, Leo had booked us each a room at a hotel only a mile from Karl Freeman's apartment. When we had pulled up to it, I thanked him, grabbed a box of ammo and a pack of rations, and then marched up to the front desk to get my key.

The room was anything but nice, but I wasn't going to complain. I'd slept aboard ships, in sewers, and in a former cultist's old hut; the room was paradise. I collapsed on the bed and allowed the night to pull at my eyes.

My dreams were of the regular variety; of that I was pleased. I'd had enough of monsters and creepy crawlies for the day, and while I loved the life I had chosen, I relished the break from them that my dreams provided.

I awoke to a light knock on the door and turned to look at the clock. It was about 10 p.m. local time. My nap had lasted just under five hours. I wasn't surprised. Even with the rest at Father Blake's, we were all pushing ourselves harder than anybody should have had to endure.

I crossed the small room and opened the door without looking out the peephole. Olivia stood there, in a bathrobe and with her feet bare. Her hair was damp and I could only assume that she'd tried the cleaning facilities out.

"May I come in?" With her robe showing off a low neckline and hugging her hips ever so nicely, it didn't take me more than a split second to step out of her way and wave her in. She looked much healthier than she had earlier. All signs of her looking ill long gone. I shut the door behind her and pulled a chair out from behind the small desk that came with the room.

As she took a spot on the bed, I sat in the chair. "To what do I owe this late night honor?"

She smiled then, and I realized then that it was the first time that I'd seen a genuine smile cross her lips. This smile left all other smiles in the dust.

"You never got a chance to tell me what Karl Freeman said." She crossed her legs, and yes, I noticed. "Did he tell you where to find the book?"

I returned her smile. "No, he didn't." I crossed my own legs and leaned back in the chair. "As a matter of fact, he didn't tell me much of anything. He wants me to meet with him again."

Concern flooded her face. "There's no time. We leave tomorrow morning." Then understanding crossed her face. "You're going to meet him tonight?"

I nodded. "Later. He said that there is much that I will need to hear tonight."

Olivia stood from the bed and the movement was slow and deliberate. She then crossed the distance between us and very slowly climbed into my lap, forcing me to uncross my legs. "How much later?"

Trust, lies, the French Resistance and Miskatonic University had no existence in my mind then. The Necronomicon be damned, in that moment we were only a man and a woman, surrounded by horrors and alone in the dark.

It was midnight when I rose from the bed and, grabbing my clothes, crossed to the bathroom to shower. I cleaned quickly and didn't let my mind go anywhere but into that soft quiet place that normally only exists first thing in the morning. It is that place where your mind has only just finished washing away the previous day and has not had a chance to look ahead at what is to come. It was peace.

I stepped from the shower, dried myself, and then dressed. I once again opted to leave the sword behind, but the holster had become a part of me, and I slid it around my waist, ready for whatever Karl Freeman might throw in my direction. While I wanted to bring the sword, I knew that now wasn't the time. I could somehow sense that it would get more than its share of blood soon enough.

As I belted the holster to my waist, I looked down at Olivia's naked form as she looked up at me. We stared at each other for almost a minute before she leapt up from the bed and grabbed her robe.

"Give me a minute and I'll meet you downstairs." She said.

"What?" I stammered, confused at first, and then Karl's words came back to me in a rush. "No, you can't come with me." She stopped, naked, with her robe only half on and gave me an incredulous look. "You will need the backup, American. He is a disciple of Cthulhu and therefore a known murderer. I will only be a minute." I walked around the bed and placed my hands on her shoulders as she tied the robe closed. "It's not that I don't want you to come. He said that I have to come alone. That," I made up this next bit hoping that it would convince her, "some truths are only for me to hear. If you come he won't tell me anything and we need to find that book."

She stared up at me and then nodded. I touched her chin and brought her mouth to mine. Her lips were impossibly soft, and I found myself wondering if it really mattered that I go see Freeman. He was only going to confirm or deny my current knowledge, and how important was that?

I pulled away from her kiss and smiled at her. As Olivia returned my smile, I remembered the real reason I was going to meet Karl Freeman: he knew something about Olivia. I hadn't admitted to myself that she was my real reason until that moment and I wasn't sure if I liked it at all. Either way, my mind was set, and I was going to visit Freeman.

"Alone. I'll be back before you know it." She nodded in acceptance and I left the room, leaving her inside.

I didn't take the car to Freeman's apartment. I had time and the walk would help me to settle my mind. It hadn't escaped my attention that the cultist could be about to tell me that I had just slept with a monster, or worse. Those kinds of things didn't sit well with many people, and would take a mile long walk before they could sit well with me.

I continued to look behind me, but even Berne was too noisy a city to be certain if the next knock on pavement was someone following me or someone just walking in the same general direction. I couldn't be certain, but I was fairly sure that Olivia would attempt to trail me to the apartment. On the other hand, the place had made her ill to even be near. She might just wait until I get back and then seduce the information from me. Depending on the revelations tonight, it might be fairly easy to do.

As I climbed the stairs to Karl's apartment, the entire building felt eerily darker; more energized. I couldn't put my finger on it, but the darkness seemed to be alive and begging to be heard.

On the third floor, I crossed the landing to Karl's door and wasn't surprised to find that it was unlatched again. I pushed it open again, slowly, just as before, expecting anything. I shut the door behind me, this time allowing it to latch.

As if he had some sort of cue, Karl called out to me once I'd stepped about the same distance into the apartment as I had the first time.

"Come in, Dr. Doran. You may see me and sit with me now. I feel much better than I did." Karl's voice was much stronger than it had been earlier and lacked any of the drier qualities.

The room was still dark as night and just as cold. The whir of the machinery was still running.

I didn't draw my pistol this time, but instead kept my hand resting on it. As I got closer to the origin of the voice, a lamp was turned on and I could see into the corner of the small room. The lamp was dim and only illuminated the table it rested on, an apparatus beside it, and two chairs facing each other.

The apparatus next to the table was the source of the odd mechanical noise, and in the dim light I watched as puffs of condensed air collected around it. This machine was responsible for keeping the apartment so deeply cold. Everything had a purpose, and I filed this information away for later.

In the chair closest to the lamp and apparatus sat a frail man. My first thought was that he was old and small, but upon closer inspection I noticed that he was only thin, as if the meat under his very skin had somehow dissolved. He was skin resting on bones, and whatever his malady, it was definitely some sort of wasting disease.

Karl Freeman was pale; even in the dim light I could see that. He wore a loosely fitting maroon robe that reminded me of Olivia back at my hotel room. He had the whisper of a beard touching his face, but it was barely existent and not as thick as mine. He trimmed it in an odd fashion with the mustache completely removed and a large dip cut into the beard directly under his cheekbones. Above those very same cheekbones were eyes that somehow told of very ancient wisdom. It was a dark wisdom, but ancient nonetheless.

All this was only noticed in the back of my mind, as the forefront was occupied with the smell. He was the source of that chemical scent I had noticed earlier. It came off him in waves and I was surprised that I could not see it.

Choosing to attempt to ignore the smell, I slowly sat in the chair across from Karl. He didn't move at all and I was concerned that he might have passed on before I sat down. He dispelled my concern by speaking.

"She followed."

I nodded. I hadn't been sure of it until Karl mentioned it then. As he said, I not only knew that it was true, but I also knew that his words that this was a room of truth were fact.

I added. "But she won't come into the building."

He shook his head. It was a slight movement and almost imperceptible but I caught it. "It is as we both knew she would, but she did not follow in the manner that you are thinking."

I got right to the point. "You said that she wasn't what I thought that she was. What did you mean by that?"

He paused before he answered and it didn't escape my notice that while his mouth moved, his face did not, as if the two were disconnected.

"Perhaps," he said, "I misspoke." He took a breath. "It is highly likely that she is more of what you think she is than anything else."

I grew angry then. "You are speaking riddles to me. That's a shifty way to lie in a room of truth."

"I speak riddles only to protect you." He blinked and it looked like it was a conscious effort. "There are certain realizations that you must reach on your own and in your own time."

I didn't respond to his words, instead choosing to mull them over for a bit. In the end I decided that if he was going to just keep riddling with me, this wasn't worth my time. I attempted to put what I knew with what he'd riddled and voiced my conclusions. "Olivia is not of the void or I would have noticed."

He nodded at my words and it looked very mechanical. "Yes. The dreams that he has sent me show me that you have a power about you."

I could sense that he wasn't going to help me in my deductions any more than he already had.

"Dreams," I shifted the subject. "Tell me about these dreams that he sends you."

Once again, Karl Freeman made a conscious decision to shut his eyes and I chose to open my view of the void energies around us. I couldn't see anything different about Karl Freeman with my sixth sense than I could without. The only thing that I noticed, and what must have allowed me to determine which apartment had been his earlier that day, was the thin fount of energy coming in from beyond the realms of this reality and touching him lightly on the neck. It pulsed in tune with a heartbeat. It was as if an intravenous solution was being pumped into this man from another world. He had no real power, but someone or something had seen it necessary to keep this man alive beyond the means of our world.

I could see that Karl Freeman had no affinity for the magical arts, but had somehow managed to anchor his soul to his body. He'd obviously had help.

"The dreams," he said after a long pause, "are those that the devourer sends to all that are willing to listen…" he hesitated, "and to a few who cannot understand their minds enough to close the doors."

I knew exactly what he meant. While anyone could study to open their minds to the dreadful imagery of Cthulhu's dreams, many suffered from those horrible nightmares simply by accident. It was believed that many who were of a creative and imaginative nature, such as artists, musicians, and writers, were open minded enough to be receptive to Cthulhu's dreams, yet not aware enough of their abilities to protect themselves. The result was that of many a creative mind being locked away in places such as the asylum at Arkham.

"Cthulhu." I said, acknowledging the name of the devourer.

"Cthulhu fhtagn!" He opened his eyes and shouted this at me, raising his hands above his head. "Glory be to Cthulhu!" This was more animated than I had expected him capable of and I was surprised.

"You seem to be a man of logic." I waved my hand at his refrigeration machine, "You're a man of science and a man who cherishes his own well-being. Why would you risk all that as a cultist of Cthulhu?"

It was a question I had asked a thousand cultists a thousand times and I'd never received the same answer. Everyone had their reasons for following the dreaded lord.

Karl hesitated longer than he had with any other statement previously, and I worried that I'd offended him. I was just about to apologize when he spoke up. "I'm flattered by your observations, but it is these same observations that led me into my current faith." He forced himself to fill his lungs again. Every movement he made looked well thought out. "If one can withstand the voice of his majesty, Cthulhu, they will discover that he whispers visions of the future, encyclopedias of truth, and knowledge beyond our wildest dreams. In the past, I, like many of his disciples, have conducted the darker, bloodier practices at his demanding. Always proudly and with the anticipation of the new dark truths that were to be revealed. I have learned," he waved his hand at the refrigeration unit, "many things through my faith."

I accepted this and shifted the subject again. "Does Cthulhu tell you where the Nazis are hiding the Necronomicon?"

Karl nodded slowly, as if he were to damage something if he moved to fast. "You mean does he know where *your* book is, not Miskatonic's? Cthulhu has said that the book has always been meant for you, and he has told me where it can be found in all points of its journey."

"Mine?" I was surprised.

"You have sensed as much. The book has always been meant for you, and only you will bring it to its full potential." Karl smiled at me then and it was an unholy thing. "Cthulhu has high hopes for your book. He dreams that it will be the final bell to wake him from his deep sleep in his sunken city."

Anger seeped into my mind again, and I did not hold it back. "He can keep on dreaming. I won't let that happen. As long as I breathe, Cthulhu will not rise."

"Time does not exist for the dreaded one as it does for you and me. He has already seen it come to pass. You cannot stop it."

My anger began to get the best of me as I barked, "Just watch me!" I took a breath then and tried to cool down. I wasn't going to let this frozen soothsayer press my buttons. "Where is the book?"

Somehow, Karl Freeman's smile grew wider. "Your course is true. You will find the book in the hands of the Traum Kult in Berlin." His smile disappeared. "They do not have it yet, but they will soon."

Relief washed over me, but not for long. The Traum Kult would have the book, but at least I knew where they were and where the book would be. I'd have to be hopeful that I could get it away from them.

I pressed him, seeking more in this house of truths. "If your lord is betting on the book opening his path back to our world, why would he let you help me?"

Karl must have been expecting this question, because he did not hesitate to respond. "For two reasons: The first is the time thing again. The book is already in all the places that it will be. Telling you where it is cannot change what will be any more than it would change what has already been. The second reason," his weird smile returned and sent a shiver down my spine, "is one of common sense. How can Dr. Andrew Doran usher in the Age and Reign of Cthulhu without the tome to light his majesty's path?"

His implication floored me. Cthulhu told him that I would be the one to summon the dark lord from his sunken sleep in R'lyeh? I would not believe it. "I choose not to believe that time is some maze with only one path to follow. Your doctrine means nothing to me."

With lightning speed, Karl reached forward and put his cold hand around my arm. "Follow me!" he shouted.

At his shout, I felt a pull that wasn't coming from him. Somewhere someone else pulled me deep into another thought, another world.

I was alone on a beach with brackish water sloshing around

my ankles. The water was warmer than I was, almost too warm. I reached down and touched the water and an oily feeling came off on my hands. The water was filled with slime and too much heat and it was unlike anything I'd ever experienced at any beach.

Crawling out of the water and onto the beach were a thousand or more worm-like monsters, each with some sort of leg protrusions unevenly distributed across its body. They were moving in a manner that was unnatural for anything I'd ever seen on Earth. The sight of them inspired terror within me and I grabbed at my pistol.

My hand came up empty and I looked down again to see that my entire holster was missing. Whoever Karl had used to call me to this land had seen to it that I don't have my gun.

I brought my attention back up to the monsters crawling around me and noticed that one of the shapeless things had seen me. It had started to slide and crawl toward me. Behind my terror I was trying to figure out where I would hit this thing to cause any damage, but I was coming up empty.

I live by one true mantra in life: If you don't know where to hit it, run away.

The brackish water pulled at my ankles as I ran up the beach and away from the oncoming monsters. Glancing over my shoulder, I realized that running might not have been the best of ideas. Behind me, the one monster in my wake had turned into ten, and he was gaining compatriots in the Great Doran Hunt.

Finally on dry sand, I kept running, making my way up the beach and up a hill. Cresting the hill I saw more of the monsters; many more. They must have been crawling from the ocean for hours, at least. I turned my head away from the sight and up along the hill further where I saw something that wasn't the usual type of monster. It was in the distance, but it was bipedal, and I was almost certain that it was human.

I had no reason to believe that whatever it was would be helpful, but it was very possible that Karl Freeman had followed me here. If he did, he might know how to convince whoever had brought us here to send us back. Otherwise, I was ready to kill him.

I ran along the top of the hill, getting closer to what I thought was Karl. I was only about thirty feet away when I realized how wrong I had been. This wasn't Karl Freeman.

It was me.

He was the same age, or at least hadn't aged much since my current point in time. If this was a possible future, it wasn't far away. This close, I could see the waves of the void pouring off him ... me ... and I stopped with one thought echoing in my mind.

I am so damned tired of fighting with myself.

I closed the gap between us more slowly than I'd approached previously, and I could see that he was holding the book; my book. He was chanting and his eyes were consumed with the pages. He didn't have any idea that I was here, and I was certain that he was more powerful than I had ever been. The book could get me home, and this Karl Freeman version of myself was certainly going to be of the violent sort. Surprise was everything.

I tackled me around the waist and knocked him to the sandy hill. We rolled down the hill together, and I noticed in the back of my mind that the creepy crawlies all over the hill moved out of our way as we tumbled.

I could feel the energy crackling off this other version of myself. He had more power than I had ever thought my body could hold, and I wondered what kind of trade-offs I must have made to get to that point.

We came to a stop at the bottom of the hill and we were both on our feet in an instant. I threw several punches to the Doppel-Doran's abdomen and doubled him over. He recovered more quickly than I expected and swung the book at me like a club. It was fast and I couldn't duck it. I hit the ground again and he was on top of me. His fists rained down on me and beat my face and chest. I managed to get a block up and shifted enough to roll out from under him. He fell off me and I managed to rise to my knees, but not before a lightning bolt arced out of his palm and into my chest. I flew thirty feet and skidded across the sand. My chest felt like a wrecking ball had smashed into it, and I was worried my heart had stopped.

I sat up with effort and watched as Anti-Andrew sauntered over to me. I was drenched in sweat, but he wasn't even breathing hard. I envied at least that.

When he reached me, he grabbed me by the hair and hit me in the jaw. He did that two more times before taking my head and forcing it to look in the direction of the ocean where a wave was cresting high.

That was when I realized that it wasn't a wave. It was the top of something. Something that pushed all sense from my mind and terrified me beyond anything I had ever experienced before. This thing, rising from the brackish water, wasn't completely solid. It moved like black smoke that stayed in a general shape. As it came from the ocean, parts of it began to coalesce into a solid mass. Its head looked like the body of a squid, and while it was bipedal, it had scaled skin like a dinosaur or giant lizard. On its back, wings protruded and came to jagged points.

Cthulhu was rising.

The reality of the situation didn't escape me. Dark-Doran had called Cthulhu from sunken R'lyeh.

I had called Cthulhu.

With the Miskatonic version of the Necronomicon.

The other me was saying something, but I could only barely notice through the terror. Whatever he was saying, it helped to anchor me back into the moment and I found the strength to drive both of my fists upward and into my other face.

He staggered backward, letting me go, and I jumped up and to my feet. I turned and ran away from the other me, but I didn't get far. A bolt of black nothing wrapped around me and halted me.

My feet were pulled from the sand and I floated in place. The other me walked around and faced me.

In a voice that was both mine and something else, he said, "Watch me! Watch as I save the world from the human filth." He returned to chanting, and in his words I could hear that he wasn't alone in my body. His chanting was being heard, Cthulhu's distant look focused on us and it was the most terrifying thing I'd ever experienced.

I could feel my sanity scratching at the last bit of will power deep in my body. I was crawling in my skin and my mind was becoming both more and less than anything or everything.

I was about to lose all of myself when I heard a voice calling out to me. It wasn't there. It wasn't anywhere, but it pulled at me.

Then I was back in Karl's freezing cold apartment and in a ball on the floor. Sweat was soaking through my clothing, causing it to stick to me.

"The future has been written. You saw the moment. Do not fight the beauty that is to become us."

Anger flashed over me. Anger at what I had seen in my own eyes. Anger at having been forced to see it. Anger that I was supposedly someone else's puppet. I stood quickly and grabbed Karl Freeman by the collar and pulled his undead face close to mine. I punched him twice and then threw him down into the machinery. The lamp fell and light flashed back and forth across the wall as it rolled. The refrigeration machine fell silent after Karl's body hit it and the old dead man panicked.

"No! Not the machine!" He began tinkering and trying to put pieces that must have come off it back into place. His hands were fast but hardly accurate and the machine wasn't going to be turning on again any time soon.

"You beast!" He bellowed. "You cannot undo what is written. It has already come to pass, you only have yet to live it!" He dove away from the machine and grabbed at something by his chair, shouting, "You need not be alive to conduct your role!" He brought up a pistol, but I was faster, I kicked his hand away and punched him in the jaw.

The rotting undead flesh broke away and his jaw fell off. His tongue flopped as he attempted to shout curses at me. I pushed him away and stomped on the remains of the refrigeration unit. He gargled and bellowed without a jaw and it reminded me of the noises the monsters on the beach made.

I grabbed Karl Freeman by the collar then and dragged him to my height. His tongue continued to flop about and I was sure that he would have been trying to bite me if he had a bottom jaw.

"As a disciple of Cthulhu and a reanimated corpse, you've been a murderer and a monster. I think that we can both agree that you've outlived your welcome in our world. What do you think?" I asked him.

His only response was "gak … gack!" as his tongue slapped back and forth.

"I knew you'd see it my way," I said. Then I reached out with my will, a considerable amount less than the other me had access to, and touched the other-world IV that was sunk deep into the dead flesh of Karl Freeman. I flexed my power, the little I had, and I snapped the power that anchored his soul to his body.

For the second time in Karl's life, he died. His body collapsed to the floor.

My walk back to the hotel seemed much shorter than the walk to Karl's apartment had been, and I was back in my room within minutes. To my surprise Leo and Olivia were both there, Olivia dressed, and both of them armed.

Leo spoke up first. "That could have been a trap. You shouldn't have gone alone."

I looked at him and then looked at Olivia. For the first time, I was seeing her through different truths, and I was unsure of what I saw. It wasn't that she couldn't be trusted, as it had been before. Now, I didn't even know what she was.

I was about to speak when Olivia asked me, "Did you learn anything new?"

I eyed her and then looked back at Leo. "I really appreciate all that you've done for me. My mission is of the utmost importance, but there are some things that we need to address before we move forward." I held up a finger. "First, while your concern is touching, it is my mission, and if I have to do something without telling you then that's what I'm going to do. Secondly, the book isn't for your Resistance. I know what you've been thinking. I'm not stupid. Once I get the book back I'm going to lock it away from anyone and everyone. That includes you. No one can use the book without becoming corrupted. I'm sorry, I know you have hopes of saving France with some tome that the Germans think is important, but it isn't going to happen." I closed my hand and dropped it to my side. "But I do need your help. I do need people to help me get into Berlin and I need people watching my back. So, I'll try to start being more of a team player, but the only thing you're going to get out of any of this is that the world won't go to Hell." I paused to let that sink in. "This is the last point where you can turn back. You can go home now, be safe, and fight your war, or you can come with me, fight evil, and risk losing more than your life and sanity. This is the last leg of our journey. Are you in?"

Leo was surprised by my words and tossed them around in his mind before saying anything.

In his hesitation, Olivia spoke up, thinking I must have meant her as well in this discussion. "I'm in."

I looked at her and snorted. "I doubt you could have said anything else." She eyed me with curiosity and I knew then that those words I said were true. If she'd have wanted to leave, she couldn't. Whatever she was, she was in this to the end.

Leo nodded after looking at both of us. "I'm in. I've seen things since we've been together to make me think that if the Nazis are not stopped your way, then they might not be stopped at all. It does me no good to kill soldiers if their dead bodies are going to continue shooting at me. I'll help you." He paused and then smiled. "Since this war started I've been helping people survive. It feels good to finally be taking the fight to Berlin."

I smiled. For the first time since I had met Leo, I trusted him.

Chapter 7: The Munich Horror

Leo had come through for us again during our exit of neutral Switzerland and getting into Nazi-proud Germany. A contact that he'd located in Berne had supplied him with German uniforms and a stolen truck in exchange for Father Blake's car. I was worried about telling Father Blake about the car, but if I didn't get into Berlin it would hardly matter what we did with his vehicle. I opted to let it go and worry about it later.

There were two checkpoints into Germany, and the first one had been easy enough to get through. I spoke to them in my best accent, not using the name of Andrew Doran, but instead of Private Hans Lukas, remembering the mad scientist from Andorra as I used it. My accent must have been passable, because we got through without much of an inspection. During the first checkpoint we had kept Olivia hidden in a compartment between the cab of the truck; we managed to get through without being searched or questioned more than our names and our reason for entering ("Orders from Lukas Herrman to report directly to Berlin."). The border patrol didn't much care about why we were entering and were more than happy to let us through.

We thought that crossing the border once had been our only hurdle, but we were wrong. There was a second checkpoint a mile up the road, and we quickly saw that they were conducting full vehicle searches, even on the soldiers.

Leo had convinced me that ditching our truck and hiking along the border until there were less soldiers was the best bet. We left the truck one at a time and managed to dive into a nearby wooded area where we could sneak away without issue. All the vehicles in front of us were lined with people getting in and out of their cars and trucks to secure and untie certain goods, and we were not noticed as we left our truck in the middle of the road.

We hiked along the border of Germany for about a day, moving very quickly, until we found a secured fencing that only had three Nazis standing near it. I was surprised by lack of guards in this area versus everywhere else that we had spied upon, and I could only guess that there was a shift change or this was an area of fence that hadn't required much defense until recently.

The three of us versus the unsuspecting three of them ended very quickly and we were in Germany. A stolen car later, and we were driving our way to Munich.

Munich was the birthplace of the Nazi party and Adolph himself had been arrested there during the party's early days. Driving into Munich, we could tell by the architecture that rose up all around us that this city was old, and my own background told me that it was medieval old.

We ditched the car we'd stolen in an alley. Soldiers were everywhere and it looked as if the populace enjoyed it. We stepped out of the car and walked into the nearest alley that we could find without being noticed too much.

As for our cadre, I hadn't spoken much with Olivia since we left Berne. I was certain that she'd managed to sense that something had changed between us and was keeping herself out of my way until she had a better understanding of what.

I didn't even know what had changed. Berne had placed many doubts in my mind concerning her: what she was, and who she was loyal to. Looking back on our time together, a lot of things were falling into place that only made sense if Olivia were working against us. Then again, a lot of things about our time together only made sense if she was what she seemed. Things like our meet up in Andorra, or our night together in Berne.

Leo was another story. I felt as though our new-found understanding of each other was encouraging us to grow closer. I didn't feel as though I had to check after him all the time, and I could trust him with tasks that I couldn't before Berne.

Once we'd dove into the alley in the center of Munich, we began working on a plan.

"The bombings." Leo stated.

"What?" I asked. "What about the bombings?"

Leo pointed at an area of the alley that had collapsed. "We'll be able to find a place to stay because of the air raids. Munich has been a major target for the bombings. There should be some places that have become condemned that we can stay in. We should be safe."

Olivia spoke up then. "But how are we going to get to Berlin?"

Leo shrugged, but I answered. "I've got a plan, and that's all that I can say for now. It's a plan in progress and when I've finished it I'll discuss it. Until then, I think Leo's plan is the best. Let's hole up in a shattered building."

This seemed to satisfy Leo, whose trust in me was growing as much as my trust in him. Olivia on the other hand didn't like it.

"If we're going to get to Berlin, we need a plan."

I rolled my eyes. "When I have one, I'll let you know. Until then, let's deal with the problem at hand, which is staying out of sight and sleeping."

Olivia continued to frown at me, but could sense that I wasn't going to budge on this. She probably could also sense that I was lying through my teeth. I had a plan to get each of us to Berlin. It was just that neither of them was going to like it.

We peeked out of the alley and into the main street before deciding that we could blend in fairly easily. We walked out and along the sidewalks, looking for a neighborhood that was bomb-shattered enough. Munich had a university and the town was crawling with students as well as soldiers. It gave it an eerie feeling, almost a familiar sense warped by war. The war had changed the face of the world, and it was felt just as much in Munich as it was almost anywhere else.

A group of these kids were laughing as we walked by, and I slowed the group so that we could overhear what could be so funny in the heart of Nazi Germany.

"He's dead?" Asked one. He was a shorter guy and probably was here because he was too short for service.

His friend, a broad shouldered man, nodded with a smile. "The hermit died last night. His son has been begging for help all day."

"Help?" The shorter man asked.

The broad man nodded again. "He keeps demanding tranquilizers and alcohol. I heard Abigail say that he was screaming about keeping the 'boy' safe."

I hoped to hear more of what was going on. I wish I could say it was only morbid curiosity but I was certain that doom had been following me since I left America. The story tickled a memory of something I had heard a few years ago, but I couldn't place it just then.

We'd been standing still for too long; Leo and Olivia were beginning to shift as more people began to glance our way.

I slung my bag over my shoulder, and remembered that Leo and I were still wearing the basic uniforms we'd acquired through Leo's contact and our wandering around with a bag over my shoulder and confused looks on Leo and Olivia's faces wasn't helping us to look very soldier like.

I attempted a last minute save and straightened, pointed toward the next corner into an alley and barked "Move," in German. I doubted that it did much to improve the perception we were projecting, but at least I tried.

We got into the alley and Olivia asked, "What did they say about a man dying?"

I shrugged. "It wasn't much. Man died, a hermit I suppose, and his son has been stealing tranquilizers." I rubbed my head. "It reminds me of something, but I can't place it."

I had no sooner said that when two men came down the alley toward us. They weren't soldiers, but they were most definitely not students.

The man on the right was large, really large. His clothing was tight and his muscles bulged to the point of his clothing looking on the verge of tearing. He had close cropped hair and a look that hadn't seen an emotion in years. The man on the left looked as if he hadn't slept in days. He was lanky with dirty clothes and wispy hair. His eyes screamed a lack of sanity.

The second man was more dangerous, and I knew this while my companions didn't. He'd touched the nether regions of the void and had come back as something more or less than human.

The smaller man raised his hand and a bolt of lightning hit me directly in the chest before I could raise a warning. I flew backward, dropping my bag in the process. As I slid across the ground, I watched as Olivia drew her gun from wherever she hid it and prepared to fire. The larger man swatted her gun away and hit her square in the jaw. She crumpled to the ground. I had no doubt that she was unconscious. I stopped sliding as Leo leapt at the larger man. They began trading blows and if my chest hadn't just been hit by a lightning bolt, I would have been impressed with Leo. He managed to get several hits in and avoid the major swings of the big guy while I was still trying to stand.

Having cast his lightning bolt at me, crazy and lanky didn't break his stride. Instead he raised his hand again. I was ready for it this time, and I raised mine, catching his next lightning bolt in my palm and holding it in a field of energy. He came at me physically then, swinging like a lumberjack. His swings arced wide and slow and I was able to duck the first two of them. His second left him open for a swing at his jaw, and I took it. He dropped hard, moaning, and barely conscious.

Leo's luck had turned while I was occupied with the littler man and now he was only standing because he was being held up by the brute.

"Hey!" I called out, and the big guy turned his head toward me. In German, I added, "He's a weak Frenchman. Why don't you try an American?"

The giant looked at Leo and then shrugged, dropping the bloodied man. He turned toward me, and I hoped my plan would work.

I let him come at me; his swing was nothing like his smaller companion's. He came in fast, and in that swing I could see pain like nothing I have ever experienced.

Somehow, I was just fast enough to duck that swing, and managed to have the presence of mind to swing in the gap he left in his own defenses. My own swing wasn't going to dent this monster and I knew that before I'd even challenged him, but I had an ace up my sleeve.

As my fist connected with the brute's side, I released the energy that I'd absorbed from his smaller partner's second lightning attack. The electrical energy exploded from my hand and the zap hurled him back and into the alley wall. He slumped next to the slowly rising form of Leo, and my companion gave his head a swift kick, ensuring that the giant was unconscious.

Leo ran to Olivia and I followed. We helped her up and already we could see her right cheek bone swelling from the knock. She seemed more or less fine aside from the blunt trauma to her face and showed none of the signs of concussion. Of this I was sure because Leo kept asking her, over and over again, how many fingers he was holding up.

Deciding that Leo could handle any sort of medical needs that Olivia might require, I stepped up to our slowly rising lanky man and grabbed him by the collar.

"Where's the book, Dr. Doran?" he shouted it at me in English, but the volume wasn't what surprised me.

"How the hell do you know who I am?" I demanded.

His only response became a chanted mantra. Loudly, he repeated, *"Are we awake or are we dreaming? The book you seek is always scheming. Screams will echo and tears will fall. Through lands of dream we see all."* He chanted this a handful of times before I shook him and tossed him at Leo. Leo eagerly accepted my shaking responsibility and set to work right away.

"The boy, he wakes. Keeper has died and the Earth quakes!" He yelled. I walked back up to him.

"What boy? What does the old man's death have to do with the Traum Kult?" The connection was there and I knew it. This man was a powerful magic user and had all but told me of his connections with the Dream Cult.

He smiled at me, and I knew then that his sanity was the price that he had paid for such power. "They hope my brother will delay you, might even be enough to slay you."

"This rhyming bullshit is getting damned annoying." I slapped him across the face. "One more time: How did you find me?"

Before he could answer there was a shake that rattled the ground and knocked me almost off my feet.

The lanky man continued to look at me as he said, "The boy is here, your end is near."

I stood and punched him in the face, sending him into the same oblivion as his larger comrade.

The ground shook again. "What the hell was that?" Leo asked, returning the conversation to French.

"I think it's the grieving son of a man murdered by the Traum Kult." I answered cautiously.

"What?" Leo and Olivia demanded at once.

I ushered them toward where we entered the alley. "We need to move. The plan is the same, we need to find a place to hunker down for the night."

Another shudder of the ground almost sent Olivia sprawling and I grabbed her, righting her. "We need to move now." I said.

In the crashing caused by the earthquakes, we found that not very many of the buildings in our currently location were structurally sound. The entire neighborhood must have been hit early and frequently by the bombings. Clean up had been ongoing, and a lot of the architecture looked complete at first glance. On second glance, we were in prime real estate for abandoned places to stay.

Leo took us into a two story building that looked like a shop on the outside, but inside was a wrecked mess. Pieces of the roof and the second flood were littered across the floor of the ground level.

Leo began to run up the crumbling stairs and I stopped him. "What are you doing? The quakes could bring the entire building down on us."

Leo indicated the second floor and then the first. "I would rather fall through the floor than let the floor fall on me." His point was compelling enough that Olivia and I were behind him in a flash.

We found a portion of the second floor that seemed the most stable and crouched down in the dark.

Olivia looked at me as we all settled down. "Those men back there were rhyming. What was that about?"

"I don't know about the larger man, but the smaller man was a member of the Traum Kult. His rhyming was meant to be a kind of scare tactic. It worked, we're still thinking about it." I answered.

Leo frowned, "If he was Traum Kult, why did he ask you where the book was? Don't they have it?"

I shook my head. "Not yet, but they will have it before we reach Berlin."

"How do you know that?" Leo asked, and I could see the question reflected in Olivia's gaze.

I hadn't told them anything about what I had discovered in Berne through the Cthulhu prophet other than the specific fact that we were on the right path; the book would be found in Berlin. I hadn't told them the rest of what I had learned because I still had no idea of how to process it myself. Explaining to my allies that it was foreseen that I would use the Necronomicon to lay waste to humanity and call up the dark lord would more than likely hinder my progress. If Leo or Olivia were to tell me the same, I'd think it my duty to stop them from ever reaching the book.

And I certainly could not tell them about the suspicions that the Berne cultist had raised regarding Olivia. He'd implied that she wasn't human and that her goals were the polar opposite of my own. My concern was in the validity of the revelation. I'd examined her humanity ... thoroughly, and I received no sense of an otherworldly presence about her. As a matter of fact, I only sensed a normal human there.

Maybe that is what should have had me concerned.

The answer I gave was, "It was part of what the cultist told me in Berne. The book would arrive in Berlin before us."

They accepted that, although Olivia's look turned slightly sour at the mention of the cultist. She'd been giving that same reaction at every mention of the cultist since we left Berne. She knew that he'd told me more than I was giving up and our relationship had lost much of the camaraderie and comfort that we'd shared before my speaking to him.

"We learned something from what they didn't say though." I provided.

Both of them looked at me with confusion and hope. "That the German's grow them big?" Leo joked.

I nodded, "That, but also that the Traum Kult doesn't know how they are getting the book." I smiled. "They only know that they are going to get the book and that I'm after it, too. Someone is bringing them the book, but they don't have a clue who it could be."

"How is that possible?" Olivia asked.

I shrugged. "Maybe it was taken by a spy, someone who was forced to keep their existence secret. Or maybe whoever is dealing with it suspects a division in the loyalty of the Traum Kult. Whatever the reason, this is an opportunity that we need to turn to our advantage."

Leo steadied himself as the building shook again. "What did any of that have to do with this dead hermit and the 'boy'?"

I wasn't sure of this myself, and worked it out verbally. "They were with the Traum Kult, but I think that this smaller man was also the madman running around Munich stealing tranquilizers." The building shook again. "I'm not so sure that the boy is actually a person. I think it might be something a lot scarier." Leo and Olivia were watching me with intense looks. "I think the hermit was taking care of the smaller man and this 'boy'. I'll bet that the Traum Kult learned what this 'boy' was and what would happen if they killed the boy's caretaker. After knowing those two things, they only had to time it for when we were in town." I shrugged. "This is all a guess, but it works with what the man said about the boy delaying me."

Screams echoed through the building that we hunkered down in. People in the streets were becoming terrified and the quakes were increasing in intensity.

Not willing to sit around during the constant shaking, we scooped up our gear and climbed down the fragile stairs before exiting the building.

In the streets people ran in every direction. Nothing made much of any sense. They didn't seem to be running away from anything, but they were definitely terrified by something, and it was more than just the quakes.

I grabbed a German man, bearded like me but with tiny glasses and no hair on his scalp, and asked him, "What is everyone running from?"

He looked about to tell me, but then a loud crash and another quake came, causing any words he was going to say to come out as only gibberish. Through his non-words, he only pointed down the street. My two companions and I looked in the direction of the pointing finger.

At first we saw nothing extraordinary. It was the street we had exited the building to, and people were screaming and running in a full panic.

Then a truck along the side of the road flattened for absolutely no discernible reason.

I dropped my bag and began putting my weapons on. The sword and the scabbard had become an extension of my body and they were on me fairly quickly.

Leo was checking his ammo as I drew my pistol. Olivia had a gun drawn, but looked too surprised to say anything.

"Andrew," she finally said, "what is going on? Is it a weapon?"

I shook my head. "Not yet it isn't."

"But what is it?" Leo begged.

"Think outside the box. Be simple. Things are rarely more than they seem."

Olivia remained quiet, but Leo answered. "It is a giant invisible monster."

"Exactly. We need to kill it."

Leo lowered his gun, looking around for a minute. "Why? If it is only a distraction from our goal, what do we care if a couple of Germans die?"

It was a good point, but I felt it necessary to clarify something that I had to remind myself of on a regular basis. "None of these people asked to be part of Hitler's war." He seemed to silently agree with that and raised his gun back up. "Besides, I think it is hunting me."

Neither Olivia or Leo reacted to that. They had obviously already come to the same conclusion.

I was nervous as I said, "I'm going to take a look at it."

Olivia asked, "It is invisible. You cannot see it."

I shook my head. "It isn't actually invisible. We humans are fragile beings and we have defenses to protect us from most of our weaknesses. The monster isn't invisible, it is only so horrible that our minds would rather perceive an invisible monster than a sanity-shattering horror."

The words 'sanity-shattering' made both of them look at me. "If I look like I'm going to shoot myself, stop me."

They sensed the sincerity in my words.

Having said my piece, I looked at where I was sure the monster was standing and pressed my finger tips to my temples, hoping to focus my concentration.

The beast stood around the same height as the buildings it walked between. Limbs and eyes and mouths met in places that should never have existed. Tentacles protruded from every orifice, pulling things in and taking them out.

I collapsed then, incapable of making the odd shapes and

misplaced limbs come together in any sort of sense. My mind threatened to fail me, and suddenly I was begging to fall into the Dream Lands. I wanted to leave my body forever and begin a life on the plains of Borea, riding the two-headed wolves and hunting the wanderers in the dark.

I was slapped then, and looked up to see Olivia's face. It made so much sense, seeing this human thing in front of me, that it was like salve on a fresh burn. The sensation of normalcy bringing shock and intensity to my burned psyche. I grabbed my head again, but kept staring through the tears at her beautiful face. After what felt like years, I could feel the burn recede, and my brain reassembled itself into something that felt like Dr. Andrew Doran.

I sat up and shook away the last of my terror.

I didn't need to tell them what I saw. They could see it through the twisting of my face.

"We need to kill it now." I said, and they agreed, but Leo stepped forward.

"It is my turn." The Frenchman said, and I wasn't sure what he meant.

He pointed at the roof of a nearby building. "You will need to go up there. With your sword and gun you can attack it from above while I attack it from below, but I need your help."

"My help?" I asked.

"Let me take a peek at it. If I can see it, even for only a second, I'll know where to properly shoot it." He looked scared, which was the correct response for what he was asking me to do.

"I've been looking at monsters like that for almost twenty years and that almost destroyed me." I pointed at Leo. "What chance would you have?"

"It is the only way to be of any good use." Leo wasn't looking at me anymore. Instead, he was watching the ground crumble under the footsteps of the monster.

"If you survive it, you won't come back the same person." It was a fact, not some sort of deep psychological analysis. If he survived looking at the monster, he wouldn't come out of it as he had been. He would be forever changed: constantly questioning all reality, touched by the void, his soul warped by the very idea of what he had seen. He could come back just as much a monster in mind as that thing before us was in body.

"I understand that, but if I come back, I'll be able to kill that damned thing with far less bullets, and hopefully not shoot you in the process." His argument was valid, and no one had allowed me a choice when I had been thrust into this world. He'd heard the consequences and still demanded to have the veil pulled aside for him.

I reached forward as he continued to look where the monster was, and I touched his temple. It was only a brief touch, but in that moment his eyes widened in terror and he fell to the ground, seemingly unconscious.

"Grab his ankles!" I shouted to Olivia. The beautiful woman grabbed him and together we pulled him backward and into the false sanctity of the building that we had just exited.

I slapped Leo hard across the face, and to my surprise he opened his eyes.

He was terrified and for that I was relieved.

His mind seemed to be reassembling itself, as only a strong mind could do. I was impressed. He seemed to be handling his first actual encounter with the other side much better than I ever had. Being terrified was the most sane reaction to what he had just seen.

I decided to give him something to focus on and thrust his machine gun into his arms. "I'm going to the roof. Shoot it and don't stop until it's dead."

Leo nodded at me, and I could see that the order had helped him. He slowly stood with his own strength as I took off toward the building Leo had previously motioned for me to take.

The building was three stories tall, and Leo had chosen well. From it I would be just barely high enough to empty my magical pistol into the creature while staying out of its monstrous reach. That wasn't my only plan, though.

Olivia was behind me as we crossed the street to the building. I knew she'd follow me instead of ask where she should go. I didn't know this because of my suspicions; I knew it because I knew Olivia. If Leo had already claimed distraction, she would most definitely choose to back me up, although I didn't think she understood what exactly my plan would consist of. If she had, I assume she would have stayed with Leo.

Before we had made it to the building, Leo opened fire on the beast. I heard him laughing hysterically as blood began to drip from seemingly nowhere above the street.

Olivia and I entered the building and began taking the stairs two at a time.

As we did so, Olivia asked a question that finally knocked loose a piece of information that I'd been trying to remember.

"Where would a beast like that come from? Why did the hermit take care of it?"

I laughed when the memory of the account flooded into my brain. "A few years ago, in America, there was a similar incident. Very similar. It turned out that the mother of the beast had mated with a being from another universe. The resulting offspring were a set of fraternal twins. One with magical powers and very human in appearance. The other was exactly the same as our monster." We passed the second floor and continued upward. "The woman then had been a cultist, attempting to create a doorway for the father of the children to enter our world, except that it didn't work out that way. This time, we have a cultist again in the form of the Traum Kult and his caring for the two. I would even bet that the man who attacked us in the alley was a brother to this creature. His power was remarkable, and if he'd had training he would have been able to destroy all of us without much thought." I was beginning to pant as we came to the third floor and then looked around for a door to the roof. "I shouldn't have left him alive."

I found the door and threw it open, running out onto the roof and looking over the edge to the pavement below.

Except that was no longer the case. Whatever the creature looked like, its blood was normal and had coated the side facing Leo.

Now, when we looked upon the street from above, it was almost as though a portion of it was being seen through a large red lens.

Nazis had joined on the opposite side of the beast from Leo and were taking advantage of his distraction as well. Together they were filling the creature with bullets. While the bullets most likely wouldn't kill the creature, it would certainly hurt, and Olivia and I couldn't have asked for a better distraction.

Olivia came up beside me and together we began shooting from above. It was perfect timing. While we couldn't see the creature, we could tell from the moving blood pattern that it had decided to do away with the pest on the ground. Our timing saved Leo from an early grave. My magical gun's bullets were doing something, but unable to see the monster, I wasn't sure what. From the wounds I caused, smoke rose while only blood came from the normal bullet wounds.

My .38 emptied quicker than Olivia's gun and once I finished reloading I put it back into its holster. Olivia didn't comment on this although it was obvious that it confused her. I took about ten steps back and prepared to run.

Olivia caught on quickly and shouted. "What should I do?"

I shrugged at her. "You'll think of something."

Then I took off with my sword gripped tightly for battle.

Leaping on top of a monster that you can't even see is probably the dumbest thing anyone has ever done. First of all, you shouldn't leap at monsters. Secondly, an invisible monster could move, and you wouldn't know until you hit the pavement in a gory mess. Lastly, you shouldn't leap off tall buildings either. This entire idea was simply dumb.

As I arced through the air, I angled my magic imbued officer's sword down with the hilt high in the air, and fell toward where I hope the monster still stood.

Luck was with me, as I jerked upward, the blade snagging and slipping deeply into the invisible flesh of the beast.

The result of my attack was unexpected. The monster screamed, but it was not with any voice. It screamed with its mind and the resulting wave of pain coursed through my own brain in much the same way that the pain had echoed on board the *Lush Delusion*. Then I'd been using the sword as well, and I wondered in the back of my own screaming mind if this was the result of using the sword on larger monsters, or if larger monsters only knew how to scream with their minds.

Using the pain radiating off the beast's scream, I intensified my grip on the sword. Somewhere deep down, I found the strength to bounce while holding the hilt, and worked to drive the blade deeper and deeper.

The result was both more and less than I had expected. Instead of going deeper, the blade began to slide along the flank of the creature, and I slid closer to the ground. I continued towards the street below for another ten feet or so before I felt something wrap around my waist.

It was one of those orifice-born tentacles, come to remove the thorn from the monster's side.

With a quick jerk of the tentacle, I was very suddenly airborne and arcing toward a building just behind Leo's new position. It was shorter than the surrounding buildings at only one story, and I crashed through a wooden roof instead of a rock wall. I was grateful for the small fortune I was granted, but the thought was far from my mind as I crashed to the floor in a shower of wood and shingles.

To my relief, I found that I had been able to keep a grip on my now blood drenched sword. I attempted to stand and collapsed, my legs not yet willing to fight the pull of gravity.

I shook my head and leaned on a nearby chair before trying again. I was able to get my feet under me and supporting my weight just as the monster let out another of his psychic screams. I clutched my head but it was over quickly.

In an explosion of what I can only assume was blind rage, the wall and roof of the building I was in blasted inward and I was narrowly missed by stone and boards as the monster came after me.

The gunfire from outside was a constant boom in the background and blood was falling like rain into the now shattered building.

The tentacle grabbed me again, and the strength with which it held me was impossible to fight. I lifted off the ground and raised my sword to attack the tentacle.

I don't know what ran through my mind at that moment. I have two theories of what happened. The first is the most mathematical: I simply calculated with my subconscious mind that the beast had to be holding me very close to its head.

My second theory was that the beast's only means of communication with his hermit of a father was through mental imagery. I was suddenly flushed with a strong sense of loneliness, of the inevitability of my death, and then I knew, without a doubt, the location of the monster's head.

Whatever the reasoning, I plunged my sword downward in front of me instead of slicing at where I knew the tentacle was.

My blade plunged deep into a soft tissue, and I knew that I had killed it. There was a shudder through the beast as its life left it. With a sudden jerk, I fell from it, pulling my sword along with me. My boots hit the floor with a thud, but I kept my balance. The tentacle slid from my waist.

Standing there, the adrenaline rushed through my head, and I allowed it to flood away all of my coherent thoughts. The first thing that pushed its way through my adrenaline crash was the collapse of stone and boards near where I assumed the left side of the 'boy' had been. Squeezing between the remains of the wall and the invisible mass was Leo, and he was shouting something.

I looked up to him and forced myself to hear the words he shouted.

"We have to leave here. We have to go now!" His face was red, and I could tell that he was still high on the adrenalin that I was currently coming down from.

"What?" I stupidly asked. The question was dumb, but behind it was the real question; why? Why now?

Somehow, the Frenchman understood my meaning and began jabbing his finger the way he had come. "The Nazis are coming."

He looked around frantically, and peered out the giant hole and up at the building I'd jumped off. "Where's Olivia?"

My ass had been kicked, but not my brain. I brought my senses back together and remembered the rest of my plan. I sheathed my sword and holstered my pistol. Through the body of the beast, I saw the soldiers running at us with their guns raised.

As Leo continued demanding the location of Olivia, I dropped slowly to my knees and put my hands behind my head. Then I turned my attention to Leo.

"Get on your knees before they shoot you."

He looked at me with his mouth agape. "Where's Olivia?"

"She'll be fine. I'm sure. Now get on your damned knees." I nodded toward the first bunch of Nazis that bounced off the monster they couldn't see.

"Where is she, Doran?" He was yelling again.

"She's not our problem. She has never been our problem." I grabbed him by the arm and pulled him into a kneeling position. "Now get on your damned knees!"

Leo's confusion turned to anger. He thought I was leaving an ally; that I was giving up and leaving Olivia to die. He couldn't be more wrong.

"So much for your plan to get us to Berlin." He said through gritted teeth as the soldiers slid in the same way that Leo had.

"No, the plan is the same. I'll get us to Berlin, and I'll get us there quickly." I gave him a half smile that I know only angered him more in the light of Olivia's disappearance.

"Oh?" Leo replied. "How?"

The next thing I said was as much to the soldiers as to Leo.

"I'm Dr. Andrew Doran. I'm an American Archaeologist looking for the Traum Kult. Take us to Berlin."

Chapter 8: The Doom That Came to Berlin

Berlin was a six hour journey from Munich, and two hours into it, Leo and I could feel every uncomfortable bump in the road. The Nazis had tied our hands and thrown us into another of their trucks. We were guarded by four of the Nazi soldiers, and after two hours of sitting in silence they had become bored. The one furthest from where we sat was nodding off, while the other three looked like they wouldn't be far behind.

My fingers had been rubbed raw during the drive as I worked at the ropes holding my wrists behind my back. It was slow going and I wasn't even sure if I'd made any progress, but I had nothing else to occupy the six hour drive.

Leo had stopped talking to me as soon as I'd demanded that the Nazis take us to Berlin. He hadn't stopped glaring at me the entire time. He'd been angry at my response concerning Olivia, and I couldn't blame him. Without explaining myself, I had left the idea open that any of my allies were easily cut off.

In French, I finally spoke up. "You look like I killed your puppy. Could you stop pouting please, before I ask them to shoot me?"

He spoke through gritted teeth. "You left her for dead."

I shook my head. "No, I didn't."

"Don't lie to me, Doran!" He was trying not to yell and give the guards a reason to hit him. "You left her in Nazi territory surrounded by monsters and soldiers." He hung his head. "That beast struck out at the building you jumped from after it threw you. We shouldn't have left her."

He was frustrating me. He should have seen what I knew long before I did. "When did you meet her?" I asked, seemingly changing the subject.

Leo brought his head back up, glaring at me as red filled his face.

"What?"

I rolled my eyes, taking pleasure in returning him some of the frustration he was giving me. "It's a simple question, Leo. When did you meet Olivia?"

His anger never left his face, but he thought on it before answering. "A few years ago."

It was my turn to keep my volume from a shout. "A few? How many is that? Was it two? Was it five?" I took a breath trying to calm myself down. "When did you meet Olivia?" I repeated.

Leo didn't like being talked to in this manner, "Two years ago."

I nodded. "Good, now tell me how you met her."

He let his head fall back as if pleading with God to shut me up. "To what end?"

I spoke through gritted teeth. "Tell me the details, Leo."

He looked at me and confusion filled the Frenchman's eyes. "I don't remember." He shook his head. "I'm not even sure that it was two years ago … it might have been three."

I returned his head shake, but with more conviction. "No, I'm sure you don't remember much about her. Actually, I'm certain that you don't remember her at all before seeing her with me."

Instead of being surprised at my claim, Leo asked. "How is that possible? I know I've known her, but I can't remember her."

I nodded. "I can't figure out why, but I think that she's … different. She might have been working against us this entire time."

Leo's anger had changed to concentration. He was now trying to figure out the same thing I was: What was Olivia? "That is impossible. She's helped us kill the Nazis."

"What's a few Nazis to convince us she's on our side?" I was looking him in the eyes. "I think that maybe the Traum Kult helped her put memories in your head so that it would be easier to convince me to accept her help. I was hesitant to accept either of you because of your Resistance connections, but both of you were able to vouch for the other and helped me to build that trust. With her there on the Kult's behalf, they were able to keep tabs on me with the option of executing me if I got out of control."

Leo laughed then, and I wasn't expecting it. "You're insane, Andrew." His look of anger was coming back. "You've been seeing monsters everywhere, and now you're seeing them in your allies."

Obviously, I was losing his confidence, and I decided to hit it a little closer to home. "Have you ever been intimate with Olivia?"

Leo's anger flared more than I had expected it to. If I was right about the Traum Kult, they may have also implanted a resistance to my inquiries into his mind. Or he was just surprised by my question. "What? That's none of your damned business, American!"

At that moment, an idea struck me. It was possible that I could get him angry enough to burn through the implanted resistance. "Don't you think that it's a little odd that such a beautiful French woman has been working with and trusting you, a relatively handsome man, for … well, supposedly two or three years, and she's never batted her eyelashes at you?" I snorted. "It took her about a week with me."

Leo's face was redder than it had been yet. He had obviously had feelings for her, and why shouldn't he? If I was right, then the Traum Kult had made her a beautiful and intelligent woman with much in common to both him and I. She was a juicy worm at the end of a very sharp hook.

Leo shouted then, "How dare you! Damned filthy American!" He didn't get much farther in his cursing. A punch from the soldier nearest to Leo absorbed much of his ire. I caught a glint of what I'd been hoping for then: his anger snapped. Somewhere inside, the magic that had been used to make Olivia believable had reached its limit.

"No," I replied, whispering now so as not to anger the soldiers anymore. "It isn't my business, but it actually is. Olivia got to you moments before you met me. I'd bet that was more than enough time to confuse your memory with a spell."

While his anger had diffused, his incredulity was putting up a solid fight. "Or you could be paranoid, Olivia could be a loyal member of the French Resistance, our friend, and you left her for dead beneath the corpse of a beast from another world."

I nodded, ceding the point. "And," I added, "out of the Germans' hands."

Realization dawned then as Leo's eyes perked up. In his smile, I saw that he had finally figured out the entirety of my thoughts. He now saw me as less of a coward, and more of a clever tactician.

I was still certain that Olivia was either an agent for the Traum

Kult or some other nefarious magic wielding group, but I wasn't stupid enough to be certain about it. Leo was correct, I had just as equal a chance of being very wrong about our French companion. If I was right about her being a spy, I'd successfully removed her from our movements, but if Leo was correct, and Olivia was our ally, then she was still free from Nazi detainment and would therefore be in a much better position to rescue us.

The smiles on both of our faces finally pushed the Nazis over the edge and the nearest soldier to me pulled a pistol from his holster and pressed it against my head. In German he added, "Shut up." I didn't need to translate for Leo. He seemed to catch on.

My lengthy discussion with Leo had also served another purpose. It had been my assumption that the ties were getting loose enough to slip out of, but by the end of the conversation I was still as secured as when the journey started. I decided at the prodding of the soldier's gun to try a new idea.

The Nazi kept his pistol in his lap after I'd taken his advice. Reaching down into the tiny well of magic I had access to, I shouted, "Ia Ia!"

Much as they had on my trip to Barcelona, my hands erupted in a blinding flash of daylight. The heat from the burst destroyed my ties. I closed my eyes as the light filled the small space of the back of the truck. Opening them, I could see that everyone, including Leo, was obviously blinded. I jumped up and grabbed the pistol from the Nazi's lap. It only took four quick shots to ensure that Leo and I were the only living people in the truck bed. I cut him loose.

The truck began to slow as soon as I got Leo free, and I knew that they must have heard the gunfire. I grabbed the dead soldier nearest to me and began undressing him.

"Quickly," I barked at Leo. "Act like you're still tied up!"

I had the soldier's clothes on as the truck finally came to a stop. With a shake and a creaking slam, I could hear the passenger side door open and shut. I pulled the canvas flaps down, so that he wouldn't see the corpses and would have to open it.

The flap swung back and before the passenger could get a good look at what he saw, I grabbed him. Dragging him into the truck, I hit him once and then twice. He was unconscious quick enough. I looked at Leo and put a finger to my mouth. "Stay quiet, I've got a plan." Leo nodded and began stripping the weapons from the unconscious soldier.

I jumped down from the back of the truck and came around on the passenger's side of the truck. I could see that the lead car had stopped about a hundred yards in front of us, and the driver was leaning out and shouting, "What's going on?"

Feeling as though I had to say something, I shouted "Dummkopf!" *Idiots!* I waved them on.

As the lead driver slid back into his seat and led the car away, I opened the door and hopped up into the cab of the truck. The driver turned to me and began to ask what was going on when he recognized that I wasn't his companion. Before he could react, I swung the recently borrowed pistol up and shot him in the face.

The lead car was just out of sight around the bend in the road, so I took the opportunity to pound on the back of the cab and then push the driver out and onto the road. I could hear Leo moving around in the back before a gunshot went off. A few seconds later, Leo joined me in the cab.

Leo had brought with him several of the machine guns and pistols of the dead soldiers as well as the bag that held my magical sword and .38 pistol. He'd also had the wherewithal to put on one of the German uniforms. It had a bloody hole in the front, but it would serve its purpose when viewed from afar.

"We are now driving a truck filled with dead Germans." Leo stated with a smile. "How did you know that it was my birthday?" I returned his smile and he added, "What is the plan now, Doran?"

I nodded to the lead car that we'd just caught up to. "Now we let our escort take us directly to the headquarters of the Traum Kult. We bust in, we get the book, and we kill as many monsters and Nazis as we can."

For the next four hours Leo and I sat in complete silence. I don't know what had caused the silence in Leo: the possibility of discovery before we arrived in Berlin, the insanely impossible odds that we faced, or confusion still over the entire Olivia discussion. As for myself, I knew exactly what was going through my mind.

The Traum Kult.

They were only slightly more than myth. Germany's own

collection of the brightest and most powerful magic users loyal to the Reich. Very little was known of them. I had no idea how many people they consisted of or what so-called deities they had allied themselves with. The only thing that I knew was a very generic sense of their power. They had a lot of it, in the way that New York City had a lot of people.

The only thing working in mine and Leo's favor was that having a lot of power didn't mean that they knew how to use it. They had no real control, and that was why the Traum Kult wanted the Necronomicon. Through their poorly translated German copy, they'd learned to step into the dreams of people from across the world and command beasts in both our world and the Dream Lands. With all their power, they'd only managed to become basic practitioners with their copy of the book. That was why they wanted the English copy of the Necronomicon.

It was probably why they wanted me.

The power itself was also shrouded in mystery. Everyone who'd heard of the Traum Kult had heard a different rumor as to how they collected their power. I was under the very vague belief that they'd each sworn fealty to one of the Great Old Ones mentioned in the book, but there were other theories. Some people claimed the Traum Kult had found out how to tap into the void itself, much like Karl Freeman had. Another popular rumor was that the Traum Kult was made completely of the oldest shoggoths, each having forgotten what it was while hiding in the shape of humanity.

I hoped the latter idea was the most true. Shoggoths were cockroaches, scurrying through the dark in search of stray souls. I'm a boot, and I love stepping on cockroaches. Unfortunately, I was fairly certain that the Traum Kult weren't shoggoths and that meant I was probably in way over my head.

That brought my thoughts around to Dean Brandon Smythe. I was willing to bet that he was planning on my not coming back from this quest of his. The idea of full access to the book was too sweet to say no to, and he knew he could offer it because I was most likely going to die in the process of retrieving it. While my death wouldn't be as ideal an end solution as actually getting the book and saving the world, the Dean probably saw it as a win either way.

If I did succeed, should I give the book back to him? That question kept plaguing me, and a week before heading into Berlin I would have had no problem with keeping the book out of the Dean's hands with just as much fervor as I was using to get it out of the Nazis'. Now that I had glimpsed a future with me bringing about the end of days, things were no longer that simple. Not to mention my theory about Olivia that I hadn't told Leo about...

I shook my head to clear it as I realized we were entering Berlin. Out of all the borders we crossed and cities we entered, Berlin had been the easiest simply because of our escort. The lead car spoke once to a guard as we slowed in the streets, but then picked up pace. When the same guard only waved us on, I nodded my appreciation and continued in line with the lead car.

We drove through Berlin for about ten minutes before I knew we'd reached the headquarters of the Traum Kult.

It was long and blocky with Corinthian columns for decoration in the front. If I hadn't sensed the rippling of power coming off the building I would have thought it a campus building straight from the grounds of Miskatonic University. It stood three stories tall and looked as though it had been built at least a century ago.

The lead car parked directly in front of the building and began to empty immediately. They were greeted by a large collection of Nazi soldiers who filed from the building and aimed their direction at us. They wanted to see the prize that was Dr. Andrew Doran.

I told Leo to get ready and then I slowed as if I were about to do the same parking maneuver.

As we slowed, I yelled, "Now!" and Leo brought his machine gun up and out the window. His gunfire cut into the soldiers of both the vehicle and the building and sent sprays of blood and chips of cement up and into the air around them. He peppered the cars and the front of the building, tearing through the front doors and into whatever lobby lay beyond.

Once I had assumed that we'd created enough chaos, I gunned it. I could see in the mirror and the few soldiers who were able to avoid Leo's attack began shouting and several jumped into the recently parked car to give chase.

I took the truck around the next corner, almost a block down from the Traum Kult headquarters. "Leo!" I shouted. "Take the wheel!" He did as I asked, and I grabbed my bag with the sword and pistol inside it. Without saying a farewell, I leapt from the truck and rolled on the pavement, hitting my shoulder harder than I had intended. I let out a yelp of pain, but came up on my feet and ducked down the nearest alley. After I had attached the scabbard and holster, I tossed the bag I'd gotten in Andorra aside, and began working my way back toward the Traum Kult.

Leo would lead the Nazis on a chase long enough for me to get into the building. Hopefully, this would keep the building undefended long enough to allow me to simply walk in, get the book, and walk out.

While I hadn't seen the side of the Traum Kult headquarters that I approached, I easily recognized it as the same building. It stank of the power of the void, and I could almost see it pouring out of the windows and off the walls.

I set about peeking into the windows and then testing them when I saw no one on the other side. Finally finding a window that slid quietly, I hopped up into it and onto the floor of the room inside.

I'd entered into a library. My head suddenly swarmed with energies and I felt almost drunk from the sensation of it all. I reached out with my thoughts and noticed that the power flooding my senses was from all the books.

I was standing inside the largest personal collection of occult and magical manuals I had ever witnessed.

I was in Heaven.

It crossed my mind, only for an instance, that maybe the power radiating from this collection of books was the secret to the deep well of energy at the command of the Traum Kult. I dismissed the idea quickly, as the power from these books was nothing to the supposed power at the Kult's command.

I had to slap myself just to get my head back into the here and now. These books, while covetous to any with my education, were not my goal. Maybe, I could come back for them…

I shook my head again to clear it and walked over to the door. Before I had even reached the door, I sensed something else, hidden in the fog of the power emanating from the books. I could hear whispers, and between the pleas for help and the promises of power, I could feel the floor and the walls surging with a different power.

This was the power of the Traum Kult, and it was begging for me to tap into it. This was an exciting turn of events and something I hadn't planned for. Coming into the home of the world's most corrupted regime of magical users was a scary prospect as only Dr. Andrew Doran, archaeologist and part-time user of the dark arts could truly appreciate. I was coming into a firefight with a pea-shooter and a large amount of stupidity. It had never crossed my mind that I could tap into the power of the Traum Kult itself.

I could feel the power surging within me, begging me to use it. I could feel why it wanted me to use it, too. It had been waiting for me, the bringer of Cthulhu to come and claim it for my own. I still had my sense of self and almost recoiled at the power's title for me.

The Bringer of Cthulhu.

They wanted me to let out the call and awake his majesty from sunken R'lyeh. My only relief came in the fact that I still felt very against the idea and the power didn't seem to care. It didn't care how I used it as long as I was willing to use it.

The downside of new power, specifically power that likes to name you and promise you fun things like world domination and unlimited everything, is that it corrupts the soul of the user. I could feel the power there, but it hadn't worked its way into me yet. Instead, it was only waiting for me to pick it up and swing it at my enemies.

I knew it was a trap, but I couldn't deny the advantage that this new found source of power would give me in the next moments to come.

My pea-shooter just became a tank.

Keeping my grasp on the power, I continued my walk to the door and pressed my ear against it. I couldn't hear much of anything and pulled the door open, only a crack.

The room I was in opened to a long hallway. I had a general idea of where I was within the building and I slid out of the room, closing the door quietly behind me. I walked the hallway until I could hear a large amount of noise in the form of boots and shouting. I came to the end of the hall and it opened into a large central room. It was the room that I was certain the stairs Leo had just shot up led to. I could see the large and grandiose doors that led outside to the street and across from them and near to me was a wide and extravagant set of stairs leading to the second floor landing.

The room was filled with beings in Nazi uniforms: men and monsters alike. I could see shoggoths, not even trying very hard to retain the human shape, standing next to soldier men proudly wearing the decorations of the Followers of Yig. Beyond them was a group of men who could be nothing other than Cthulhu cultists. The self-mutilation of their own bodies overly evident through the blood stained uniforms they wore. Beyond the Cthulhu cultists, the fishmen of Dagon stood wearing only trousers. Across their pale fish chests they had crudely painted swastikas resting adjacent to the Eye of Dagon, a crudely drawn etching meant to symbolize the eye of their parent.

This collection of monsters was exactly as I'd feared when I had interrogated the bartender in Andorra. That many normal soldiers would normally be an issue, but that many beings from the dark arts made this entire idea seem almost impossible.

I could hear the power of the Traum Kult whispering to me, promising me that these monsters would be nothing before my might. I knew that sooner or later I would have to deal with most if not all of these beasts, so I let the power continue its whispering and allowed it to bolster my ego and confidence.

I was about to do something incredibly stupid when a voice reached across time and chilled me to my spine.

"Where is Dr. Doran?" Lukas Herrmann, the Nazi scientist from Andorra, shouted. He was storming his way down the stairs, his flesh incredibly pale. His pace brought him directly in front of the Cthulhu cultists and he slapped one of them across the face. "Something is terribly wrong and you stand there, barely conscious." He turned and directed his attention to everyone in the room before shouting in German, "Everyone, chamber a round and be ready for anything. The Traum Kult would not be happy if Dr. Andrew Doran were to just walk in here."

As if on cue, a loud slam came from the front doors and a large number of human soldiers stormed in, pushing along a bound Leo.

The marks on his face implied that he'd given them a damned good fight before they brought him in. He was also bleeding a little from his temple. I was happy that he was still alive but I was equally concerned that Lukas Herrmann might not want to keep him that way.

My surprise at seeing Herrmann there was swept away in the conversation that followed.

A human soldier stepped forward and told Herrmann, "We were able to overtake the truck and seized this Frenchman."

Herrmann looked Leo up and down with the same regard that someone might look at the mess a dog had left on the carpet. "Any sign of Doran?" He directed his question to the soldier who had spoken, without taking his eyes off Leo.

The soldier didn't move as he said, "There was no sign of him, sir."

Herrmann took his eyes away from Leo and poked the soldier in the chest. "Form a perimeter around the building. I don't want him thinking that he can just walk in here, I want him dragged in." As an afterthought, Herrmann added, "Don't kill him unless he doesn't give you a choice."

The soldier nodded and began barking orders to the rest of the soldiers that had followed Leo in. Herrmann jabbed Leo in the chest and stated to the soldiers holding him, "Follow me. He will be useful."

I watched as the soldiers keeping Leo in line dragged him up the large staircase in the wake of Lukas Herrmann.

I pulled myself back down the hall a little ways until I was confident that I wasn't going to be seen for a while. The monsters were still all guarding the main hall and I'd have to go through it to get to Leo. I looked down at my hands and realized I was shaking.

It wasn't anger or adrenaline; I was surprisingly calm. It only took me a moment to realize that it was the power of the building surging through me. It wanted me to use it so badly that it was practically dragging me into the fight.

I drew my sword and pistol and decided that there was no reason not to listen to the magic.

I stepped forward into the main hall and threw a curse at the door that the Nazis had dragged Leo in through, locking it and reinforcing it with a wall of magic. The curse would keep people, or other things, from flanking me in the moments to come.

The surprise of my appearance was enough to allow me two quick cuts with my sword, taking out the gun arms of the nearest two soldiers. I had assumed they were the only humans in the room, but their limbs both melted at the magical sword's touch, and they fell to the ground writhing in pain.

The barely held together shoggoth stood nearest to them, I leapt at the same time it did. As it jumped at me, it let go of the wavy human form it had chosen as well as the Nazi uniform, and came at me in a fully tentacled mass of teeth and eyes. I could feel the magic surging through me and allowed it to guide my movements. The monster's teeth-covered tentacles lashed out at me, trying to take chunks of my neck and arms, but I brought the sword down on every attack, cleaving its slimy arms. Each tentacle melted at the sword's touch puddled in a steamy stench on the floor.

Two dead Nazi soldiers and a writhing and dying mass of shoggoth parts are about as far as I got before the Cthulhu Cultists, several other shoggoths, and the followers of Yig all raised their machine guns and opened fire.

On pure reflex, I put my hands in front of me and projected a magical shield. The energy rippled around me. Normally, the power of my shield would be enough to deflect a poorly aimed spell, but nothing direct. With the power of the Traum Kult behind me, I was completely surprised by the power of my shield as it deflected and stopped bullets from a large collection of machine guns. It wasn't going to last indefinitely, and I could already feel the strength in the shield beginning to wane, but I was greatly impressed.

The gunfire let up just as my shield was about to collapse, and I didn't hesitate. They all dropped their guns and ran at me en masse.

In one fluid motion, I drew my magical .38 and fired three shots. The first two shots take out two cultists, each in the head, while my third shot barely missed a shoggoth.

Three Children of Yig reached me first and each was wielding a barbed short sword. The blades were lined with gold and ended in a large barb. The length of each blade was covered in sigils etched in gold. I'd have loved to have time to examine each of the sigils on the swords, but they were moving much too close to my flesh, and I decided to save it for another time.

I deflected the first blade with my magical sword, simply slapping the blade aside, before the second came in at my waist. I spun quickly with the momentum of the first attack and parried that blade away as well. Still spinning, I caught the stomach of the third Yig worshiper with the edge of my blade and removed him from the fight before he had even entered it. I slapped the first attacker in the face with my sword, slicing him as it connected, and then stabbed the second through his chest before his hooked blade could sink into my shoulder. While the first still clutched at his face, I brought my blade out of his companion's chest and swung back around, taking off the first's head.

I turned back toward the rest of my attackers, slightly surprised that no one else had joined in the fight, when I saw the Cthulhu Cultists chanting and holding their arms high above their heads. I looked down and realized that I had noticed all this too late. The granite floor had liquefied and tentacles were coming up and out of it, searching around for me. As if that wasn't enough, the follower of Yig who I'd disemboweled was standing back up, a vacant look on his face and the sword still in his hand.

The floor-tentacles were still searching for me when he attacked. He might have been mostly dead, but he fought with a zeal that he hadn't had in life. I blocked three of his swings but only barely, as he brought his barbed sword toward my face. I slapped the sword away and brought mine forward to cleave his head, but missed by inches as the floor-tentacles found my waist and leg, dragging me toward the liquid granite.

Frustrated, I realized that I still had my pistol drawn and took aim at the tentacles. I was about to pull the trigger when the magic whispered in my mind again. Instead of firing, I barked a spell as loudly as I could.

My world lit on fire. That's how it looked, anyway. My body was covered with magical flame that didn't hurt me or my clothing, but blackened the tentacles instantly. As the floor monster writhed and let me go, I tumbled and then leapt for the undead follower of Yig, grabbing him tightly and hugging him too closely to allow him a chance to bring up his blade. I let go of the undead monster when I was sure that he wasn't going to be getting up again and allowed the flames to die away as I turned toward the cultists and the two shoggoths.

I brought up my pistol and placed two bullets into the shoggoths. I was only facing the cultists now.

My pistol was still drawn, and I had one bullet left in the six shooter. I quickly shifted my aim from the dead shoggoths to the nearest cultist and pulled the trigger. I holstered it as I watched the bullet bounce off the cultist's own magical defenses. His magical strength was much less than mine, and I saw this as the reverberation from my one gunshot made him reach for his head, and staggered his charge.

His fellow cultist came at me with a fist that radiated a dark purple energy. I was still holstering my gun and couldn't bring my sword up on the side he was attacking quickly enough. I was going to need a magical defense. I hadn't even thought it and the same shield that had deflected so many bullets sprung up around me and caught his power-fueled fist. The fist connected with the shield right next to my temple and the magic in his assault gave it enough force to shatter my shield and drive me to my knees.

I sprang back up from my knees and punched at his face with the pommel of my sword. I didn't use any magic for the attack as he had, but he didn't put up a shield and I shattered his nose.

I had allowed myself to be distracted by the first two cultists and now the third, still about ten feet away, brought his hands up. A lightning bolt, larger than I had seen from the practitioner in Munich, leapt from his outstretched hands and came at me. I caught it in my arm and the jolt of it sent me into the air.

I don't think that I hit the ground, but am still unsure. I know that at some point while I was in the air his two companions had joined him. I was hit again and again by magical lightning bolts and continued to twirl through the air until I came to a wall shattering stop near the hallway I'd entered from.

I was surprised I was still alive. Those blasts of energy had numbed my arms and my head was swimming with pain. Pieces of the wall were still falling down on me as the three cultists approached.

Somewhere in my tumble, I'd let go of the sword. I figured, in the part of my brain that could still handle figuring, that it was for the better. I'd brought a sword to a magic fight. It was time for me to bring out the magic.

I reached down with my power. Down into the stone floor and into the rest of the building. I tapped the power that the Traum Kult had loaned to me through my mere presence in the building, and then I tapped their electricity. I filled myself to the point of overflowing and opened my eyes.

Somewhere in my reaching for the power, I'd stood up. I didn't remember doing it and I hoped then that it intimidated my enemies as much as it had creeped me out.

Their looks told me that they hadn't felt me collect all that energy, or else they just didn't think that it'd be enough. "The Kult wants you alive," the nearest cultist said in English. "Don't make us kill you."

Something inside of me was really enjoying this showdown, so I replied, "I would love to see you try."

They smiled, obviously hoping that I would have put up a fight.

Their hands tingled with power and it was the only hint that I was given about the upcoming attack. It was more than I needed.

When they'd hit me earlier, I hadn't been ready for the attack, but this time I was more than prepared.

Their lightning blasts combined into one deadly spell and came at me in the blink of an eye. The bright light lit the whole room in a sort of flashing effect. The blast hit me in the chest and I just stood there, taking it.

Taking all of it.

I did to the cultists what I'd done to the magic and the building: I absorbed the power. I took all that they would give, and they kept pouring it into me as if adding more power to their attack would overwhelm me. If I'd have been in my right mind, I would have thought the same, but the magic whispered to me and told me to keep it up and that I'd be alright.

It wasn't long before I'd taken most of their strength and all three of the cultists collapsed to their knees.

I was bursting with energy and the walls and floor were getting zapped by the excess as it rolled off me. I felt as if I were going to explode, and I probably was about to, until I saw the cultists as something more than what they were.

Kneeling on the floor in front of me weren't just some mad and blind worshipers, they were a portent of the future. Before me were Cthulhu Cultists, the very people who I'd be helping, possibly joining, if that future I'd seen was going to happen. It angered me that they planned to usurp my life and make me some messiah of the damned.

It filled every magical ounce of me with anger, and I wanted to release it at them, wiping the world of them and hoping that they took my projected future with them.

The power released, sending a torrent of electrical energy out of me like a wave. I didn't aim it or try to direct it, I only released it. As it left me in a powerful current, it swept over the three cultists and completely destroyed their bodies. The granite floor was covered only in ash when the lightning had finally dissipated.

Energy still coursed through me, but I could tell it was taking its toll as exhaustion consumed my limbs.

I saw my sword laying across the room on the floor and I retrieved it. I could feel the curse that I placed on the door beginning to weaken. A lot of someones were on the other side and were giving it their best to get through the door.

It would have been a waste of time to try to repair the curse, so instead I ran up the wide staircase to the second floor landing. I had only just touched down on the second floor when the curse snapped and the front door burst open. I didn't have time to count how many were there, but it was easily more than any magical shield I could conjure would be able to handle. In a rush, I ducked down the hallway and sprinted, hoping that I was going in the direction that Leo had been taken.

As I ran, I checked doors, trying to open them. I finally found one that was open just as the soldiers reached the second floor. I ran through it and slammed it shut, throwing another quick curse at this door, hoping that it would hold long enough to get me to wherever I needed to be to get to Leo.

The room that I'd chosen as my refuge was an office, but it was definitely a Nazi supporter's office. The wall to my left as I entered had a book shelf at the nearest and furthest ends of it with the blank section of wall in between the shelves covered with a Nazi flag. Across from the bookshelf wall was a wall with photos in frames. On cursory glance, I noticed Lukas Herrmann in some of them and wondered quickly to myself if this might be his office.

I decided it couldn't be, as there weren't enough occult items in the room. As a matter of fact, there were none.

Directly in front of the wall with photos was a large wooden desk and a leather chair. On the other side of the desk, and basically in the center of the room, was a chair facing the desk.

Sitting cross-legged on that chair was Olivia, wearing the same outfit I'd first seen her in when I'd met her in Andorra.

Her face was filled with relief upon seeing me, and I only barely registered it as I stepped into the room and decidedly ignored her to examine the rest of the room.

"Oh thank God!" She declared. "You're here. I thought I'd die here."

I ignore her, running past her and to the Nazi flag. I tugged on it experimentally and then yanked on it, pulling it down.

During this, Olivia stood up and put herself in my peripheral vision. I pressed on the wall, continuing to ignore her, and checking the density.

"Look at me, Andrew." She begged in French. "We need to get out of here. If you can secure me a gun, I think that we can get to Leo."

I began chanting at the wall, pressing my hands against it harder and harder, filling my mind with the magic and projecting it directly into the wall.

"Listen to me, American! Why are you ignoring me?" She slammed her hand on the wall next to mine and I didn't even flinch at the outburst. "I heard them say that they were taking Leo to the third floor. They are going to interrogate him about you."

I looked at her for the first time then and my look must have scared her, because her eyes widened. "What room?"

She opened her mouth slowly before answering. "I don't—"

"What room?" I repeated, cutting her off.

She became indignant. "I said I don't—"

In a flash of movement, I drew my pistol and aimed it at her head. She had no way of knowing that it wasn't loaded, and her face exploded in terror.

"I'm sure," I started, "that you 'don't' do a lot of things." I pressed the barrel of the pistol into her forehead. "For example. I'm sure that you don't eat, you don't sleep, and that you don't breathe." I forced the pistol forward further, jerking her head backwards. "You *don't tell the truth!*" My face was flushed with anger as I focused on how much I hated the deceit that this woman represented. "Most importantly, you don't exist. You're a phantom, a manifestation, or some sort of projection!"

Instead of retaliating, screaming, or pulling away from me, Olivia only frowned, and a tear leaked from her eye and down her cheek.

She tried to force a smile, but she was obviously upset. "I was hoping," she said with a strained voice, "that I was going crazy, but it seems that you came to the same conclusion that I did."

I could see that it upset her, and while I didn't think that she had real feelings, I still felt uncomfortable about it, and holstered my pistol. I turned back to the wall and resumed my chanting. In seconds, the wall finally started to ripple like a puddle and my hands began to sink through it.

I kept chanting as I pulled my hands away and then I jumped through.

The puddled wall solidified as soon as I was on the other side. The room adjacent to the office was a large bathroom with a bathtub and sink. I ran to the door and turned the latch quietly, hoping that the soldiers who were most definitely pounding on the door to the other office wouldn't notice. When I turned back around, Olivia was sitting in the bathtub, her arms wrapped around her knees and tears were streaming down her face.

"What am I?" She whispered.

I quickly reloaded my pistol, dropping the spent cartridges on the floor. As I finished loading the pistol, I attempted to answer her.

"I have a few theories." I holstered the gun and ran to the window, it was nailed shut. I drew my sword and wedged it under the jam and began working to loosen the window. It wasn't a huge window, but it looked large enough to just barely fit me and my accoutrement of weaponry.

"My first theory," I continued, "is that you're a projection sent from the Traum Kult. I think they sent you to aid me in getting captured and to Berlin. It would also allow them to track me really easily." The window lifted a little, and I kept working the sword. "This theory, I don't believe only because there are much easier ways of tracking me. Besides," I looked at her just to verify my statement, when I did so, I opened my sight to the magic. "You don't have any of the void on you. Meaning that the magic of the Kult didn't spawn you."

I could suddenly hear a crash from the room next door and the stomping of Nazi boots crossing it.

"My second theory is silly at best. It's possible that you're a ghost or phantom from the Dream Lands and that the Night Watchers sent you to me. That makes even less sense because the Night Watchers think that I'm dead and, once again, you don't have the void on you."

I pressed a little bit of magic into the window and it began to budge a little more. It wouldn't be long now. I could hear the crash of the shelves and some sort of glass shattering from the room next door. They were getting frustrated and were about to search elsewhere. My time was short.

"The final theory that I have scares me."

Olivia had stopped sobbing and from behind me she asked, "What is it?"

"When someone looks into the void, the dark recess between the dimensions, their minds try to apply sense to it. It doesn't work. Everyone who looks into the void loses their sanity in the attempt to make sense of the insensible. Everyone, without exceptions and in varying degrees. Leo saw the beast in Munich for only a split second and I can guarantee you that in some small way his sanity has worn away." The door to the bathroom suddenly erupted in banging as the soldiers tried to get in.

I hurled another locking curse at the door to secure it and increased my furious working of the window.

"I've looked into the void more than I care to admit." I continued over my shoulder. "Specifically, I used it only a day or so before I met you to save the Captain of the *Lush Delusion*. Instead of accepting the shattering of my sanity, I created you, but I'm not stupid and you had to be real. My insanity was projected through my connection to the void magic and you worked yourself into the memories of Leo and introduced yourself to Father Blake and the primitive minds of the undead Nazi soldiers who kidnapped you." My memories all clarified as I realized the truth. It was only me shooting at the Nazis while they tried to kill a projection that wasn't even real. It was all a deluded strategy built by my insanity. I needed a means of getting into Andorra, so my insanity supplied one. "You're my insanity made manifest. A disability with access to the subtler levels of my magic."

The nails finally slid free of the jam and the window lifted open. I could feel the curse on the door beginning to shatter already and didn't hesitate to climb out of the window. I grabbed a pipe leading up the side of the building and started climbing the wall, placing my feet on the few bricks that stood off the wall slightly more than the rest.

As I climbed I continued to talk, knowing that a phantom from my own imagination could probably hear me very well no matter how much distance I put between us.

From below me, I heard Olivia ask, "What happens to me now that you know what I am? Do I just vanish?"

"No," I grunted as I climbed. "Knowing I'm insane doesn't cure the insanity." I grunted and moved upward another foot. "Besides, I think you're a safety net. Your existence is an outlet for my insanity. If you went away, I might turn into a dribbling mess. Talking to myself is preferable." I was almost within reach of a third floor window and lowered my voice. "Whatever the hell you are, you're handy to have around."

"How so?" She was calling to me from somewhere above me now.

"Well, if Leo is on the third floor, then you're privy to information that I'm not. Somehow you've tapped into the void enough to have answers to some of my questions."

I reached the window and realized that it was closed. I stretched upward to peek through it and slipped on a brick. I almost fell and the terror leapt to the forefront of my mind. I grabbed the nearest brick and struggled to regain my footing. Once I thought that I was secure enough, I tried again to peek through the window. This time, I was successful.

This time, I did find the office of Lukas Herrmann. He stood behind a desk similar to the last one that I'd seen. He was leaning on it as the soldiers spoke to him.

"He was here, sir. He killed some of the Traum Kult's guard."

Herrmann interrupted them with a slam of his hands on the desk. "Where did he go?"

The guard looked terrified. "We lost him on the second floor. We assumed that he ran into a bathroom, but the window was nailed shut. He just vanished."

I almost leapt out of my skin as Olivia's voice whispered in my ear. "You're welcome."

I whispered back, lowering myself from the window. "You closed the window?"

"Right after you told me that I could be useful, I realized that I like being around and that if you get killed then I get killed. So, stop being stupid, American, and cover your tracks."

I smiled and pulled myself back to the window. Herrmann had stepped out from behind his desk and was jabbing one of the soldiers in the chest. "Dr. Andrew Doran is a practitioner of the arcane. Take me to where he disappeared."

More than happy to get out of the office, the Nazis filed out of the office with Herrmann trailing behind them.

The moment his office door shut behind him, I tested the window. It wasn't locked or nailed shut, and slid open easily. I pulled myself into it and landed lightly on the floor.

I had just gotten to my feet when the door swung back open and Lukas Herrmann walked in.

I didn't hesitate because I knew that he wouldn't either. I drew my pistol and swung it upward to plant bullets into his chest. Somehow, he was across the room and before me in a moment.

Herrmann slapped my pistol from my hand and I didn't watch as it slid across the floor of his office. Instead, I drew my sword. I was about to swing it when Olivia was suddenly standing beside me.

I was distracted and Herrmann's fist smacked me in the chest. It was like being hit by a truck. Even the lightning from the cultists hadn't hurt like that. I was launched across the office but I managed to stay on my feet.

"Sorry!" Olivia shouted. I shook it off, even though I was worried that my heart might have stopped and stepped back toward the German. "He's dead, by the way." Olivia added.

"What?" I asked, forgetting that Herrmann could hear me until he raised an eyebrow. I ignored him, instead listening as Olivia repeated herself.

"Take a second and look at him. He's got a touch of the void. It's subtle magic, but just look at his flesh. He wasn't this pale in Andorra."

I looked at Herrmann again, and this time I looked carefully. Olivia was right; he was very pale. With that, he was also moving very stiffly. The touch of the void she mentioned, I'd originally ignored. Herrmann made no point of hiding his love of the arcane and the Traum Kult, and I'd mistakenly assumed that was what I had seen. Upon closer inspection, the magic worked its way into his flesh. It was a locking spell, and it was meant to keep life in a deceased corpse.

"When did you die?" I asked him.

He smirked and I realized that his face wasn't moving anywhere near as much as it should have been. It was only more evidence of the undead.

"You shot me when you were in Andorra." He answered. "When you were escaping in that damned hotel. I took a bullet in the stomach." Herrmann lifted his shirt then and showed me a hole that was still in his necrotic flesh. "I died of an infection a day after you escaped." Just barely above the bullet hole were the magical runes cut into his flesh. That was what had brought him back. "The Traum Kult, in their infinite wisdom, knew that they needed the great Lukas Herrmann as he was, not as a mindless drone. They dragged my soul back from the pits of Hell and locked me into this body." He flexed and I could have sworn that he almost doubled in size as he did so. "I will be the gatekeeper who ushers in the demons who will destroy the lesser races."

Herrmann gave the Nazi salute, and I took the moment to step forward and plunge my sword into his chest, knowing that the magic of the sword would kill him: a creature of the void.

My sword plunged deep into Lukas Herrmann's chest, and in reaction he jerked and twisted away, surprising me and taking my sword with him. I didn't mind. If he was going to leave a magical, body-melting sword in his body, who was I to argue.

I stepped back and watched as he continued his jerking reaction and came back around to face me.

Instead of a look of pain or terror on his face, Herrmann was smiling. I grabbed the hilt, thinking to put some of my will behind the sword's power, but when I touched it, I sensed that none of the sword's magic was touching Herrmann.

Herrmann wasn't sitting still during any of my revelation.

Instead, the moment that I grabbed the sword's hilt, he punched me in the face twice.

I fell back, feeling the blood leaving my nose as my vision exploded with stars. I was still standing after the second hit, but a slap from Herrmann's open hand sent me sprawling across his office.

Herrmann looked down at the sword protruding from his chest and smiled at it. "Is this…" His smile widened and he gently pulled the sword from his body and looked at it like … well, like I would have looked at an artifact such as the sword. "It is. Dear God, how did you find this magnificent American relic?"

I brought my knees underneath me and struggled to stand. "You know," I grunted. "It kind of just fell into my lap."

"Idiot." He whispered. "Do you know what this is?"

I finished my slow ascent to a standing position and answered. "The Blade of Captain Fitz." I nodded toward the sword. "I'd assumed that was what it was, but I wasn't going to bet on it until I saw your reaction."

The undead mass that was Lukas Herrmann brought his eyes close to the blade, examining every inch of it. "Forged in the fires of the blood of his enemies and with metal found in a crater. It was blessed by your natives to corrupt the beast of other worlds." He looked at me. "They say that nothing foreign to this plane can stand its touch."

That was my answer. "It didn't hurt you because your body and soul are from here."

Herrmann nodded. "Yes. I am different from the other undead things. Those bodies are home to demons from the other realms, mine houses only me." He swiped twice with the sword and then looked at me. "This will be a prized addition to my collection." I stepped forward and Herrmann brought the blade up quickly, placing the tip underneath my chin. "I thank you."

This enraged me. Of course he was going to add it to his 'collection.' Herrmann was a Nazi, that's what they did. They saw the world as their big toy box, and if something was in it that they wanted they would take it. It was disgusting and wrong. Somewhere these damned Nazis had gained the idea that it was their birthright to claim the world.

Magic filled my fists and I asked through gritted teeth, "Where's the book?"

Herrmann tilted his head, as if confused by the audacity of my question. "The Traum Kult wants you alive. They didn't say that I couldn't kill you first."

During all Herrmann's drooling over the sword, he hadn't seen me unclasp the scabbard from my belt. Before he could plunge my own sword through my neck, I batted the blade aside with the scabbard and then stepped in tight to the decomposing German. Once I was closer, I had to act quick if I was going to stay ahead of the preternaturally fast Herrmann. I thrust my fist forward and punched the Nazi in the abdomen.

It wasn't a normal punch and carried with it as much magic as I could focus into my fist. My hand went through Herrmann's stomach and deep into his guts.

I pulled my hand from his abdomen and guts streamed out with it and onto his office floor. His face was contorted with his anger as he brought his free hand down in a reflexive action to collect his spilled entrails.

It was just the opening that I was looking for and I planted my still-magically charged and blood-covered fist into his face. Once my hand was deep inside Nazi brains, I released the magic.

Herrmann's skull exploded outward, showering his office in blood and brains.

He fell and I kicked the sword from his grasp. I walked over, picked it up and returned to him. His body was flailing about as it fell to the ground and that spoke volumes for the spell that had locked him into his body. He wasn't housed in his brain like the rest of the undead things I'd dispatched. Instead, Lukas Herrmann was literally housed in every inch of his body.

I wasted no time in hacking him up and I was covered in blood in a matter of seconds. In less than a minute, I'd had the writhing corpse of Lukas Herrmann dismembered into about fifteen large chunks. I kicked them across the office and even threw the head itself outside, just in case they decided to try to wriggle back together or melted … or something.

I don't know everything that could happen. I'm not the Necronomicon. Some stuff is just weird, and surviving it means planning for the weirdest. Sometimes that includes throwing a mostly exploded head out of a third floor office window so that it can't reanimate.

I allowed myself a breath and realized that Olivia had never really vanished during any of that fight. She'd just been standing quietly in the corner. I felt like that must be an analogy for how our relationship would progress from here on out; Olivia hiding out in the corner of my mind until she has something to say.

Finally getting my breath under control, I looked at her. "Any suggestions?"

My own personal phantom stepped away from the wall and came closer. "Leo is on this floor. Lukas would want to have kept him close." Olivia turned away from me and walked to the door. She grabbed the handle and opened it and I almost yelped at her that someone might see her when I remembered that this was all in my head.

In reality, Olivia hadn't opened the door and she hadn't just stepped outside and looked around. What really happened was that my subconscious had just reached out with my magical affinity and scanned the hallway. Damned insanity. I'd have to keep reminding myself of that if I wanted to not scream every time Olivia opened a door or stood up in a hail of gunfire.

She came back in and took her time carefully shutting the door again. As if she'd heard my thoughts, which she very well might have.

"I don't know which room has Leo in it, but outside the door and down the hall are four soldiers. Lukas must have thought that you would go after the book before going after Leo." She pointed out the door and to the left. "The soldiers to the left are looking down the stairs, waiting for you to come up." She brought her hand slowly to the right, indicating the other length of hall. "The other two are facing this way, they look like they're waiting for Lukas to come back."

I was once again placing a lot of trust in something I didn't understand, but now was not the time to start doubting my course. I replaced my scabbard and slid the sword back into it before stepping up to the door and pulling it open quietly.

Stepping into the hall, I didn't even look left, instead drawing my pistol and firing at the two soldiers who looked right at me. After the report of my pistol echoed through the hall, I spun and shot the two remaining soldiers as they turned and brought their guns on me. My bullets took the first one in the head and the second one in the chest. They both dropped.

My gunshots wouldn't have bought me any time and I was willing to bet on soldiers racing up the stairs at that moment. I began throwing open all the doors adjacent to Herrmann's office. I came across a locked door and stepped back to kick it when a yell from down the hall made me bring my pistol up.

Olivia was about four doors down from me. "He's in here! I can hear him!"

I sprinted to her and tested the door. It was locked just as the last one had been. My boot rose and fell through the door with a crash that jolted my entire body.

Inside sat Leo, tied to a chair with his face bloodied. Beside him is another soldier watching over him. I dove to the side as soon as I kicked the door open and managed to avoid the bullet that would have surely taken me in the chest. Out of harm's way in the hall, I prepared a spell and sent it in ahead of me. The light drained from the room, except for immediately around my target, and I killed him quickly.

Returning the lighting to how it was, I ran over to Leo and cut him free with the sword.

Leo thanked me quickly before saying, "The Necronomicon is in the basement with the Traum Kult. Herrmann has sent all the guards down there to protect them."

I rolled my eyes. "Of course they're in the basement. It wasn't going to get easy any time soon."

I took the guns off the corpse and checked them both before handing them over to Leo who went ahead and checked them again.

Leo took up a position next to his chair and I eyed him curiously.

"I heard one of the soldiers saying Herrmann was headed back this way."

I shook my head at him. "No, he isn't heading anywhere for a while. I took care of him." Leo smiled at that and returned to standing. "But you're not wrong." I continued. "There are more soldiers between us and the basement than I think that we can handle."

Leo raised his eyebrow and smirked. "More than you can handle, maybe."

I laughed. "Fair enough. Either way, it'll be very difficult to get to the basement of this ridiculously large building."

The mirth subsided and Leo nodded agreement. "Then what is our plan?"

Olivia popped into existence beside Leo. "I think that I can help you with that, but it will hurt you, American."

Leo almost leaped out of his skin but he recovered quickly and threw his arms around Olivia.

My eyes went as wide as Olivia's did. We were both surprised as Leo said "I told you that she was on our side." He stepped back from her. "Thank God that you are alive."

I pointed at Olivia. "You can still see her?"

Leo's look turned confused. "Of course I can see her." He turned to Olivia. "How did you get to Berlin?"

Olivia ignored him and looked right at me. "I'm as surprised as you are. I'm not trying to be seen."

"What?" Leo asked. "What do you mean 'trying to be seen'?"

Olivia poked Leo in the chest and watched him rock backward and then conducted the same experiment with me. The results were the same.

"Is it because he looked into the void?" She asked me.

I nodded slowly. "That's the only explanation that I can come up with." I pointed at her and raised an eyebrow. "You *are* a figment of my insanity, right?"

Olivia returned my nod. "Once you realized it, I realized it also. I live inside your head."

Leo held up his hands. "What?"

Olivia and I both stopped ignoring Leo and turned to him. "Andrew, what is going on?" He asked.

Olivia answered. "I'm a figment of Andrew's imagination. He looked into the void too much and I'm the result of his magical side going insane."

Leo looked incredulous. It wasn't that he didn't believe it so much as he didn't want to understand it. Finally, he said, "This is all too damned much."

Olivia held up her hand. "Too much or not, I might be able to help you both get to the basement."

"You can?" I asked. I was ready for any sort of break.

"Yes. We can walk through the void." Any sort of break, except for that one.

I shook my head. "Walking through the void is what created you. Thanks, but I don't need any more brain trauma. There's barely room for the two of us."

Olivia shook her head. "Looking into the void hurt you, but you wouldn't be looking into it. I would guide you."

Leo was confused. "But I thought you were a part of him."

Olivia nodded. "I'm a piece of his subconscious with direct access to his magic. Whatever I see will actually be his interpretation of what he senses in the void."

"Meaning that I can teleport through the void, like a shoggoth." I was excited.

Olivia frowned. "Maybe."

"What do you mean maybe?" Leo and I both asked.

"You're still human and your brain won't be able to take prolonged exposure. If this works, we can't make a habit of it."

I nodded slowly, but it was an absent nod. I was suddenly renewed with faith in our ability to get the book. This looked like it was something that we could actually accomplish.

It dawned on me, but only for a second, that I could still be very wrong about Olivia. She could instead be some sort of trick to drag me into the void and leave me there.

I'd decided earlier not to care, and that thought left as quickly as it had arrived. I just didn't care if she was a threat. She'd proven herself this far, and I was done guessing about it.

"Let's do this." Was all that I had to say about it.

Leo nodded. "I'm done talking about this. I want to shoot something. Many somethings."

Olivia grabbed us both by the arms. "Close your eyes. Don't open them until I tell you to, and be prepared to shoot."

I gulped. Leo had no idea what to expect from the void. There were terrors that lived outside of visibility. We were not completely protected, and I was certain that Leo had no idea what that really meant.

I closed my eyes and felt the wave of nothing engulf me. It was a feeling that brought terror and anger and a shuddering sense of falling in every direction.

The void is outside of reality, and therefore very difficult to describe.

I heard screaming followed quickly by the whimpering of what sounded like a wounded animal. It continued for a short eternity before I realized that it was me and shut my mouth. There were images in my mind that I knew weren't just images, but creatures of thought, abstract ideas reaching toward my soul to taste the thing that had entered its world.

Surprisingly, I figured that I must have been getting some sort of deep protection from Olivia, because the last time I'd teleported through the void I had been much more terrified.

"Open your eyes." Olivia shouted. "Leo is down, protect him."

I stood and almost fell over with nausea. I brought up my pistol and saw that I was standing behind two soldiers who were walking away from me. They were walking toward a huge door and we were in a hall lined with stone blocks.

In front of the door stood six other soldiers. These two were on their way to join their companions. I lowered my pistol and drew my sword, choosing to save the bullets. With Leo out of commission, I was going to need every bullet in the six shooter.

One fast swing of my magical blade dropped the head of the soldier in front of Leo, before he could register the looks of surprise in the other German's eyes. I pulled my sword back to myself and then thrust it into the chest of the soldier in front of me.

Holding him there as he slowly died, I brought my pistol back up and took aim at the soldiers in front of the door.

I called over my shoulder. "How's Leo doing?"

"I'm here." I heard, only barely, through his tears.

I fired two shots at the soldiers and thanked whatever being might be listening that Leo had finally come to his senses as one bullet went wide and the second found its mark in one soldier's chest.

An explosion of sound erupted beside me and my hearing said goodbye. I spared a glance to my left as the soldiers fell in pairs and I saw Leo opening up with his machine gun.

When I looked back the soldiers were all dead in front of the large door.

I pulled my sword free of the soldier and pushed him to the ground before waiting for my ears to return to me.

When I could hear again, I turned to Leo. "That was easy."

He smiled, but his eyes were screaming with mental anguish.

Olivia's voice appeared in my head. "I only had the reach to protect your mind from the beasts. He will heal, but it might take time."

I slid my weapons back into their respective homes and then slapped Leo across the face. "You're in the real world now. There are monsters out there, but I need you here and now. Are you a child or are you Leo; the Killer of Nazis?" His eyes seemed to leave whatever terror that they could still see and come back to the basement we stood in. He looked me in the eyes and forced a smile. "I am here." He went through the motions of checking his gun and it seemed to bring him back almost completely to his old self.

Almost.

Leo, as I had known him, was gone. Every encounter with the void would introduce me to the remains of Leo. This was his second trip and the effects of the horrors of other worlds on my friend would be revealed in time.

He nodded at me when he'd finished checking his gun and together we stepped over corpses and came to the door. It was layers of wood with a large ring down the center of it. We gave it a tug but it was obvious that whoever was inside had barred it.

Before I could ask, Olivia whispered in my ear that she couldn't get us into the room or see into it. I glanced at Leo and decided that it was probably for the best.

I stretched out with the still strong sense of power and realized that it was all coming from this room. All the power that I had been using had been coming from this central room. The Traum Kult had decide to hole up with the source of all their power.

They were holding it, almost hugging it, as if they were trying to keep it all to themselves. This was most likely the case, but they didn't have what I had.

The power wanted me to use it. It wanted me to be the adult to take the power from these children and own it.

So, I did.

They resisted with what was probably all their strengths, but I was the stronger.

I blew the door off its hinges and into pieces, sending it scattering across the room inside. Leo and I stepped inside the room as one and readied our weapons.

No amount of readiness could have prepared me for the surprise of what I saw.

The room was small, but made so by the adornments on the walls. The walls were covered by metal, shined to mirror like quality and each foot of it was trailing a bundle of cables. Each one of those cables came down and directly into the arms of one of five people lying on tables in the room. There were two men and three women, all wearing nothing but these wires from the walls. In the center was a man watching monitors, paying absolutely no attention to me as he spun dials and pulled levers. Each movement that he made caused a twitch or a hint of an emotion across the face of one of the five.

I could feel the power coursing through those cables and down into each of those bodies. They were collecting magic and funneling it into the Traum Kult. The Dreamers of Germany were feeding on magic.

Sitting next to the man was the book. The Necronomicon rested on the same platform as the levers and dials that the man spun.

I wasn't looking at the book, my goal for the last week. No, my attention was on the man.

"Dean Brandon Smythe? That explains how they got the book."

The Dean glanced over his shoulder, giving me a passing glance. "One moment, Doctor. I'm almost done." He hit another lever and then turned to face me, picking up the book.

"What is this?" I demanded.

The Dean of Miskatonic University, the man who put me on this quest of the damned, answered, "A recruitment drive."

"What?" I asked. Leo stood next to me not understanding any of the English, but waiting silently for my signal to attack.

"To put it simply, the Traum Kult have put together an engine of magical collection and distribution. That," he held up the Necronomicon, "with this, makes them the most powerful beings on the planet." He hugged the book to his chest and stepped closer to me. I didn't miss that he stayed just out of sword range.

"With all his power, you'll be able to harness and control all the monsters and beasties that you love so desperately to fight." His face twisted in a half smile that didn't seem at all natural on his face.

"I will, huh?" I rolled my eyes. "You expect me to do this while working for the Reich?"

He shook his head. "With all that power, do you think you'd really be working for anyone?"

I ignored that statement and waved my sword about, indicating the wiring coming from the wall. "This is all just collection. What's the source?"

The Dean's smile turned darker and suddenly it fit his face. "The Nazis." He shrugged. "Not the Nazis directly, but from the POW camps. Every time the Germans gas or mass execute people, there's a member of the Traum Kult standing by and funneling all that life energy directly to the Kult headquarters."

I gagged and almost threw up. Leo saw this and raised his gun higher, preparing to end the Dean's life.

"Don't let it get to you, boy." The Dean was speaking to me with sympathy in his voice and I almost gagged again. "The Germans are going to kill them anyway. We're only collecting that power and using it to come out on top. You've seen it in all of your studies. Civilizations rise, and to do so they must step on the lesser civilizations. The Traum Kult is rising," he hesitated, "and we want you to lead us."

I straightened. "Give me the book."

He reached out and handed it to me. I assumed it was a trap and reached very slowly for it. When nothing happened, I grabbed it quickly and flipped through the pages, making certain that it wasn't a fake.

It was the real thing. I now held the American translation of the Necronomicon with all of its additional secrets and spells.

I looked at the Dean. "Why would you give it to me?" He shrugged and folded his now empty arms. "I told you; I'm hoping that you join our cause. You can't kill off the Traum Kult, we're scattered all over the globe. You're certainly not leaving the same way that you came in. The Nazis are on their way here en masse and you will not be capable of fighting your way through them all. You're tired and wouldn't make it."

I sighed. He was right, and I'd tried not to think of how we would escape up until now.

The Dean continued. "I don't want to put it bluntly, but I will. You can join the Traum Kult and lead us into glory, or you and your friend can die here."

Dean Smythe had me cornered. I could lead Leo into certain death, or I could fulfill the prophecy as I had seen it in Berne. I could become the Bringer of Cthulhu.

That image shook me to my core. I shuddered involuntarily as it came to the forefront of my mind and I saw it all again. There I was, standing on the beach as writhing inhuman beasts crawled and slid across the sand. Cresting the waves was a terrible shape, both solid and gaseous with horror rising off it as if it were steam. I could hear the words as I chanted them, reading directly from the book—

The book.

I had another option.

I looked at Leo and smiled. In French I said, "Don't worry. I think that I know what I'm doing"

"You think?" Leo asked. He didn't take his gun or eyes off Dean Smythe.

In English, I said to the Dean. "Smythe, I've decided to fulfill a prophecy."

He smiled, misunderstanding what I was saying. "Really? I'm glad to hear it."

"I don't think you will be, actually." I held the book back out to him. "When I last saw you, I told you that the day would come when I put you down." I let the book drop. "That day has come."

The Necronomicon hit the floor with a loud slap that drew the Dean's attention. His five cultists all sat up abruptly and glared at me with hate. With the Dean's eyes on the book, his friends were the only witnesses to my bringing the magical sword down onto the cover of the tome.

A psychic scream ripped through the room and I gritted my teeth through it, pleased with myself for guessing right. The book was as much a piece of the void as the piece of the reef from Innsmouth had been. It had been made in our world, but had been used and changed by the void. It had become alive and my sword was melting it.

I was also pleased with myself for another reason.

I had changed the Cthulhu prophecy. If there was no book, there would be no summoning of the dark lord.

The Dean was screaming, both in pain and in anger. His eyes bulged as they looked at me accusingly. I expected his eyes to burst from his head, and I wasn't disappointed when Leo pulled the trigger to his machine gun and made it happen.

The book had almost completely dissolved now and the scream was getting weaker. Still connected to the cabling, the Traum Kult members began hurling spells of lightning and fire at Leo and myself. I deflected them all with my will power and found it very easy to do.

The power still had hopes for me and had decided against abandoning me after my betrayal.

Or maybe all those lost souls were begging for retribution.

I preferred to think the latter.

In a matter of seconds the room had been reduced to a bloody mess. It wasn't until the smoke had cleared that I realized Leo had been giving me a pained look.

"That book could have changed the world." I could see the Resistance dying in his eyes, but he had no idea what this book really meant to humanity.

"Yes, and that was why I destroyed it."

I stood there for a moment, looking at the carnage surrounding us, and gathered my wits. I was tired, but the magic continued to surge through me. I needed to destroy this room, but first I needed Leo's help.

"Start pulling these wires off the bodies. I need them."

Leo looked at me in horror, but I ignored it and started about pulling the wiring from the nearest bodies. After a moment of just standing there he came back to himself and helped me.

His look of horror returned when he saw me attaching them to my own body, but he didn't slow in his work and was soon helping me to stick them to my skin.

"What are you going to do?" He asked me in almost a whisper.

"He's going to give me the juice to get us out of here and destroy this place." Olivia answered from behind the Frenchman.

Leo shook his head. "I cannot go back in there."

Olivia quieted him with a touch. "It won't be like last time. With this much power I can protect you both." She looked at me. "With this much power he doesn't really need me, I would think."

I looked at her as Leo finished attaching the wiring. "Actually, I would like the few shreds of sanity I have to remain in place. So, if you don't mind, get ready to get us out of here."

Leo looked around at the walls. "What about this place? How are you going to destroy it?"

"That," I answered, "is my job." I quickly created a ball of energy between my hands. Inside it you could see lightning bouncing around and desperately attempting to get free and wreak havoc.

"I'm the only thing holding this energy together. As soon as we vanish, it'll destroy this room, and maybe more." I looked to Olivia. "Are you ready?"

She nodded and touched Leo and me.

It had been a week since we'd magically teleported out of Germany, and I was sitting in the former Dean's library and drinking the former Dean's scotch while Leo sat across from me.

I hadn't expected Olivia to take us all the way back to Arkham. Leo's love of the Resistance meant that he needed to be in France, and I would have expected Olivia to understand that better than anyone. Her response when I asked her about it was that she'd read Leo's mind, and now that he knew of this other world, he would be considerably depressed to return to fighting only Nazis.

Because 'only Nazis' isn't enough?

I accepted it and Leo never brought it up. As a matter of fact, he'd decided to start learning English and I'd been helping him for the last two days.

Idleness wasn't in either of us, so we'd started coming back to the school. When the administrative board had inquired as to where their Dean had gone, I didn't hesitate to tell them that he'd been discovered to be a Nazi spy. They didn't believe me until they saw Leo's stern look. At which point, they decided that they needed a new Dean, and who better to fit that role than an Alumni with a Doctorate. I threatened decapitation, but they wouldn't listen. They said they'd handle the major decisions and that I could feel free to join in on discussions at any time, but the University needed a Dean, even if he hated the idea.

This specific moment in … my … library, drinking my scotch was one of revelation.

"She's standing right next to you.""Still not see here." Leo answered in broken English. I was making him only talk to me in English to aid in the resurgence of the little bit that he'd already known.

I looked at Olivia. "Maybe this means his mind is healing?"

She shrugged. "Or that the magic I used to convince him I was real is wearing off. There is no way to know for sure without speaking directly to someone else who had seen me, and Father Blake is a little out of our way."

"What she says?" Leo asked.

"She shrugged." I smiled at her.

I was getting antsy to show off what I'd found, and switched to French to tell Leo. My fingers scratched at the folder beneath them.

"Do you know what this is?" I asked rhetorically.

He shook his head.

"This report is a firsthand account by a Dr. William Dyer of this very University. In it he describes terror and horror like we've never seen." I smiled. "He also goes on to describe a battle between two major races of long ago."

"Battle?" Leo asked, sensing where this was going.

"I think this is the largest known collection of alien weaponry on the planet, and I have reason to believe that Brandon Smythe gave a copy of this account to the Traum Kult."

Leo smiled, my excitement becoming mirrored in him. "When do we leave?"

"In one week." I downed my scotch and poured another.

"Where is it?" He pressed.

I gave my newest companion and friend a bigger grin than I'm sure he'd ever seen me produce. "We're going to Antarctica."

About the Author

Matthew Davenport lives in Des Moines, Iowa with his wife where he enjoys biking, drinking, reading, podcasting, geocaching, DIY'ing, and writing. Only once in a while does he do it all at the same time. He writes and reads a little bit of everything. His writings have been mostly short stories, with Random Stranger being his first novel.

You can keep track of Matthew through his twitter account @ spazenport.

Bibliography

Short Fiction:

Guard Dog
Hate to Fly
Sherlock Holmes and the Case of the Murderous Confidant
Lerdrin's Rings
Black Friday
Evolving Faster than Light

Novels:

Andrew Doran at the Mountains of Madness
Random Stranger (Abstract Series 1)
Stranger Books (Abstract Series 2)
The Statement of Andrew Doran
The Trials of Obed Marsh
Broken Knights
The Sons of Merlin

Curious about other Crossroad Press books?
Stop by our site:
http://store.crossroadpress.com
We offer quality writing
in digital, audio, and print formats.

Enter the code FIRSTBOOK
to get 20% off your first order from our store!
Stop by today!

Made in the USA
Middletown, DE
25 June 2021